Ice Cream and Intrigue
A Nanny Blu Cozy Mystery

Summer in Diamond Bay
Book 3

By

Maci Grant

ISBN: 0692577750
ISBN-13: 978-0692577752

TABLE OF CONTENTS

CHAPTER 1

Blu stared out the window at the clear summer sky. It was another perfect day. The kids dawdled over their cereal while Blu took a few minutes to savor her coffee.

The relative peace was shattered by a quick knock on the door, followed by its being immediately thrust open.

"Guess what!" Maddie whisked her way into the kitchen with her two charges right behind her.

Twelve-year-old Brennan scowled as usual, and ten-year-old Chrissa looked as if she'd just stepped out of a magazine, with more accessories than Blu could count.

"Do you know what today is?" Maddie asked, her eyes wide with excitement.

Blu looked up from the coffee that she sipped. "Apparently it's a good day." She smiled at her best friend.

"Let's see...what is the best day of summer in Diamond Bay? Think about it. Think about it." She tapped her foot.

"Ice cream day!" Joey jumped up from the table. In the process he knocked over the remainder of his cereal. The bowl crashed to the floor with a splash.

"Oh, Joey." Blu frowned and rushed to get a towel.

"Sorry, Blu." Joey sighed and danced from one foot to the other to avoid the puddle of milk.

"No! No sad faces on ice cream day!" Maddie waved her hands through the air. "Okay, so we're all going to have one of these." She handed out hats that featured a scoop of ice cream with sprinkles on top. "This way everyone knows that it's officially ice cream day."

"I can't believe that you remembered." Blu laughed as she tossed the towel and plastic bowl into the sink.

"You did tell me many times that it's your favorite time of summer. Since you hadn't had one yet, I thought the kids and I would join in. I hope that's okay."

"Of course it is." Blu gave Joey's shoulder a squeeze. "And Maddie's right, no sad faces on ice cream day. Take your sister and get dressed, okay?"

"Sure!" Joey grabbed Marley's hand and pulled her down the hallway. "It's ice cream day, it's ice cream day!"

"Ice cream, ice cream!" Marley shrieked with the kind of exuberance that only a four-year-old can muster.

"Can you give them a hand? It will get us to the ice cream a whole lot faster." Maddie smiled at Brennan and Chrissa.

"I guess." Brennan shrugged.

"I'm fixing Marley's hair!" Chrissa ran after the

younger kids.

Once Maddie and Blu were alone in the kitchen, Maddie stepped closer to her and lowered her voice. "I'm sorry for springing this on you. The kids' dad has a court date today and I just wanted to do something to cheer them up."

"How are they doing?" Blu frowned. "I forget sometimes that they are going through that."

"I think they're okay, but you know how hard it can be to tell with them."

"Yes, I do. I think it's a great idea that you're doing this. It's the perfect day for it."

"Great." Maddie smiled. "I have the treasure hunt all planned too."

"Wow, Maddie. I'm impressed." Blu finished her coffee and set the cup in the sink.

"I've learned everything I know from you." She laughed. "I just hope that I don't forget where I hid anything."

"Let me just get a few things together and then we can start the hunt!"

Blu was eager to participate. It was even more fun that she didn't have to plan it. Every summer she would declare an ice cream day and take the kids on a treasure hunt that would eventually lead them to their favorite ice cream shop. It was a great way to fill the day, and the kids loved the challenge of the hunt even more than they loved the ice cream.

Once she had everything she needed, she returned to the kitchen to find Maddie surrounded by eager, ice-cream-starved children.

"Alright, alright, let's go!" Blu laughed.

She and Maddie led the kids down to the beach, which was only a few steps away.

"Okay, my hunt might not be as good as Blu's, but all that matters is that it ends in ice cream, right, kids?" Maddie grinned. "The first clue is hidden somewhere on the beach!"

"What? That's it? No other hint?" Chrissa flipped her hair over her shoulder. "That's ridiculous."

"It'll be fun!" Brennan started to run off across the sand. "At least it's something to do."

Marley held up a bright red plastic shovel, ready to dig. Joey cupped his hands and dug in the sand also.

"Ready, set, hunt!" Maddie laughed and waved her hands through the air.

As the hunt began Maddie and Blu hung back while the children raced across the beach.

CHAPTER 2

"I'm really surprised you did all of this, Maddie," said
Blu.

"I took a page out of your book." Maddie smiled.
"You know, when you first suggested that I become a
nanny, I thought you were nuts. Who would want to
spend all of their time with kids? But now I think I get it.
Sure, it can be difficult, but it can also be a lot of fun."

"You basically get paid to play. What isn't fun about
that?" Blu grinned as she dug her toes into the sand. "I'm
glad you gave it a try. If there's one thing that's great
about kids, it's that they never let you stay down in the
dumps for long."

"That's true. Every time I start to think that I can't go
another minute without losing it, one of them will do
something so absurd or adorable that I remember that
this is the best job in the world."

"I can agree with that." Blu grinned. "Although
sometimes I still wonder what it would be like if my first
career choice had worked out."

"It still could, you know." Maddie studied her with a sympathetic smile.

"Maybe. But I don't know. Everything changes so quickly, and I'm so out of touch with the newest standards. I still like to write my family newsletter to keep my brood in touch—that seems to satisfy my journalism bug."

"That's like running your own magazine with all of your brothers and sisters." Maddie laughed.

"That's true. The family reunion is coming up. You have to come."

"Hm—I wouldn't mind seeing your oldest brother again." Maddie lifted an eyebrow.

"Maddie!"

"What? I'm single now."

"So is he." Blu shook her head. "He's chronically single. Every time he gets serious about a woman he takes off to some new country to find himself."

"I can't blame him there. Sometimes I wish I had done that instead of rushing into marriage. You know, when we're kids it seems like something to hope for—the loving husband, the cute little house, maybe a baby to cuddle, but that's not what it is at all. Or at least it wasn't that way for me, I guess."

"I wouldn't know." Blu frowned. "Look at us. You regret taking the plunge, I wonder if I've missed my chance to even take the plunge."

"Oh please, Blu, you have plenty of time. People fall

in love when the time is right for them. You can live a life of untainted freedom and then decide to try out settling down in your eighties. That's my new plan. Unless of course your brother wants company on his next excursion."

"Maddie! Gross! Have you ever smelled his shoes?"

"Nothing a little air freshener can't fix." Maddie gave her a playful shove. "Don't worry, I'm just joking. Besides, you and I are already promised to someone else. Remember?"

"Huh?" Blu looked over at her. "What are you talking about?"

"Please, don't tell me that you don't remember Alexander Dreme."

"Oh! Alexander Dreamy!" Blu laughed so loud that the kids stopped digging through the sand to look up at her. Then they returned to their hunt. Blu thought they might dig up the entire beach before it was over.

"He was mine first."

"No, he wasn't. He tripped on your shoe and landed in your lap. That was a total accident, not an introduction."

"All I'm saying is that I saw him first."

"Do you remember those sketches he would draw?" Blu grinned. "We thought he was going to be famous."

"I wonder if he is. I'll have to look him up."

"Do you think you can find him?"

"Are you kidding? With social media I can find

anyone."

"You have skills, lady."

"If I find him, I'm not going to tell you though, or you might try to steal him."

"He was mine first." Blu laughed. "Remember the water fountain?"

"You cut in line in front of me! Otherwise it would have been me that he bumped into!"

Maddie and Blu were laughing so hard that they didn't even notice that the kids had centered in on one area.

"I found it!" Joey shouted. He plucked a clue out of a pile of sand. It was a bright orange piece of paper. "Follow the trail of shells to the brightest bum on the beach."

"Maddie?" Blu laughed.

"I didn't say I was as clever as you." Maddie grinned.

"Beach Bum!" Marley pointed toward the bar in the distance. "Beach Bum!"

"You're right, Marley. Good job!"

The kids tore across the sand toward the Beach Bum.

"Hm, I wonder if AJ is having his annual brunch today?" Maddie smirked.

"Oh, you do think you're quite clever, don't you?" Blu bumped her elbow into Maddie's.

"Innocent!" She ran off after the kids.

Blu trudged along behind them. "I think I've created a monster."

When they reached the Beach Bum there were plenty of cars in the parking lot. A banner hung over the entrance of the bar that declared the annual brunch for all of the local leaders of the community.

"But where's the clue?" Joey looked around. "I don't see anything."

"The brightest beach bum." Brennan frowned. "Maybe we have to look for a bright butt?"

"Brennan, it's bottom." Marley huffed.

"Oh, Maddie, you didn't." Blu looked over at her friend.

"He agreed to it." Maddie grinned.

CHAPTER 3

Blu and Maddie stepped into the bar with the kids right behind them. Several large buffet tables were set up in the middle of the room. AJ stood in the center wearing bright orange pants.

"That's pretty bright." Blu raised an eyebrow.

"I was going to go with the yellow, but it washes me out." AJ turned around and smiled at them. "This is for you." He held out four tickets to the kids. Each snatched one from his hand.

"Thank you!" Marley smiled.

"Anything for you, princess." AJ reached down and ruffled her hair.

"That's it. You found the golden tickets." Maddie clapped her hands. "Now you have to follow the path to the ice cream shop."

As the kids began to scramble for the door, Blu started to follow after them.

"Blu, wait," AJ said. "Can I talk to you for just a second?"

"I'm sorry, I have to catch up with the kids."

"And I have a bar full of hungry people that think they are important. But I just want one second. Please?" He smiled.

Blu turned back to face him. It was the first time today she really looked him in the eyes. "What is it?"

"Hi." AJ grinned at her.

"Hi?"

"How are you?"

Blu smiled. "I'm good. How are you?"

"Wonderful now." He winked at her, then walked back toward the bar.

Blu's smile grew wider as she headed out of the bar to catch up with Maddie and the kids.

The path to the ice cream shop was part of the challenge as well. It usually included obstacles of some kind. Maddie stuck to tradition by having the kids climb up over a sand dune.

"Clue!" Marley shouted. She picked up a sneaker and waved it in the air.

"No, that's not a clue." Maddie shook her head.

"Marley, put that down, sweetie. Someone must have left their shoes while they went for a walk in the sand." Blu walked up to her.

"If they did, then they're probably limping, because there's only one." Joey laughed. "Maybe it's a one-legged pirate."

"You know, there are some people that have only one leg. You shouldn't joke about it." Chrissa crossed her arms.

"Alright, alright, let's just put it up here so that whoever lost it can find it." Blu set the shoe down on the wooden walkway beside the sand. "Don't we have an ice cream shop to get to?"

The kids gave up on the special path and raced for Peddle's Ice Cream Shop. It was their favorite place to have a treat.

Marley pushed open the door. "Ice cream!"

Mr. Peddle laughed from behind the counter. "Well, hello there, kids. I guess you want some ice cream?"

"Yes, please." Joey grinned.

"I like your hat." Mr. Peddle winked at Marley. "Look what I have." He held up a cake knife that was decorated to look like a slice of cake. "My wife bought it for me. Isn't it great?"

"Yes!" Marley reached out to touch it, but Mr. Peddle drew it back before she could.

"Careful there. It's very sharp. Just to look at—not to touch, alright?"

"Sorry." Marley frowned.

"It's quite alright. Now what kind of ice cream would you like?"

As the kids gave their orders Blu spent some time looking through the choices herself. One of her favorite things about Peddle's shop was that he always added a few new flavors.

"I'll take the berry cherry chocolate," Blu decided.

"What kind of berries does it have in it?"

"Only raspberries and strawberries, I'm afraid. Is that okay?"

"Sure. I just thought there might be blueberries."

"No, that's one flavor I don't carry." He laughed.

Blu was curious as to why he didn't carry blueberry ice cream, but she was distracted by directing Marley not to eat the sprinkles straight out of the toppings bin.

"What are you going to have, Maddie?" Blu asked.

"I don't know. Hm. I think the mint chocolate chip. That's always been my favorite."

Mr. Peddle prepared ice cream cones for them both.

Once each of the kids had their ice cream, they settled at a table. Peddle's Ice Cream Shop wasn't very big, despite being a very popular summer destination. More than once, they'd been to the shop when there was standing room only. Despite this, Mr. Peddle never made any effort to expand.

"Enjoy, kids, enjoy." Mr. Peddle disappeared into the back room.

While he was gone Blu looked through the photographs that hung on the wall. There were several of Mr. Peddle and his wife. She was a petite woman with wild curly hair. Over the years the hair had turned gray, but the curls were still wild.

When Mr. Peddle came back out of the back room, Blu walked up to him to give him an extra tip.

"Oh, thank you, Blu."

When he took the money Blu noticed that his right hand shook a little.

"How is your wife, Mr. Peddle?"

"Oh, Martha? She's wonderful. She's started her own crafting booth at the mall. I think she really enjoys creating."

"What a lovely idea. I will have to go see her booth sometime."

"I'm sure she would love that. I think that the summer crowd is a bit too busy on the beach to get into the mall."

"Oh, just wait until the sales start." Maddie grinned as she walked up to them. "Then the beaches will be empty."

"That's very true." Blu nodded. "But they'll still be back for ice cream."

"They better get all they can this year. I'm not so sure we have another year in us."

"What?" Blu's eyes widened. "You're thinking of closing?"

"Well, I'm not getting any younger. I think maybe it's getting to be that time." He nodded as he rubbed his hands together. "Nothing is final yet, but there's a lot of pressure on me to sell. I'm starting to think that if he wants it so bad, maybe I should just let him have it."

"Has someone been harassing you?" Blu frowned. "I could talk to Chief Pitman about it."

"Oh no, I wouldn't want to involve him in anything.

The chief has enough to do. Besides it's not harassment, it's just smart business. I'm in no mood to fight; I'm sure he knows that. Martha and I could use a few years with nothing to do. Our lives have been so busy that I've barely had the time to appreciate her the way that I should."

Blu smiled at the sweetness of his words. She wanted to comment on it, but just then Marley came running up to her with ice-cream-covered hands.

"Oh boy, let's get you washed up."

CHAPTER 4

Blu walked Marley out of the shop and around behind the building to the bathroom. It was in a separate small building and was the shared responsibility of a few different small shops in the area. With its proximity to the playground, it was also used by those who didn't want to walk to the bathrooms near the beach.

Marley squirmed as Blu cleaned her face.

"Oh, don't do that or the tickle monster will get you!" Blu grinned and tickled Marley under the chin. Marley squealed and squirmed even more. Soon she was tidied up.

Blu met up with Maddie just as the older kids stepped out of the ice cream shop.

"Since Mr. Peddle mentioned it, why don't we spend some time at the mall?" Maddie smiled. "Have cash, will spend!"

"That sounds like a good idea. We can have a late lunch there." Blu glanced back once at the Beach Bum, then joined the others on the walk back toward the beach house and the cars.

As they walked, Blu noticed a man who walked as well. It wasn't too unusual to see people walking the same path, but it was usually people who were on their way to the beach. This man was dressed for a business meeting, not the beach. She noticed that he had a briefcase with him as well.

She paused and watched as he walked toward the ice cream shop. With a shake of her head she turned and followed after the others.

When they arrived at the mall it wasn't very crowded.

"Please can we play in the arcade?" Joey begged.

"I want to too." Brennan smiled. It might have been his first smile of the day.

"Alright, go ahead and get some tokens." Maddie handed Brennan some money.

Blu walked Joey and Marley up to the counter to buy some tokens.

"Blu, do you mind keeping an eye on Brennan? I think Chrissa wants to check out Poppers," Maddie asked.

"Sure. I don't think Brennan will miss that." Blu smiled. She watched the pair walk into the bright pink, glitter-covered store.

As the kids played in the arcade Blu people-watched. She swept her gaze up and down the corridor in search of Mrs. Peddle's booth. She didn't see the booth, but she did see Mrs. Peddle.

Blu started to wave, but the woman was caught up in a conversation with a younger woman. Blu noticed that the younger woman clenched her hands into fists. A moment later she raised her voice.

"You lied to me. You both did!" She spun on her heel and stomped away from Mrs. Peddle.

Blu looked away before Mrs. Peddle could spot her. She knew that there was likely something wrong between the two and she didn't want to get in the middle of it. Still, she wondered what they might be arguing about. Mrs. Peddle was not the type of person that she'd expect anyone to be angry with.

Blu was distracted by Joey running up to her to ask for more tokens.

When Maddie and Chrissa returned, they both had sparkly bags.

"You found some things too, I see?" Blu grinned.

"A girl has to beautify, right, Chrissa?"

"Sure." Chrissa giggled.

"Blu, have you ever thought about sprucing up a bit? A little eyeliner wouldn't kill you."

"It might." Blu grinned.

By the time they got back to the house that night the kids were very worn out. Blu prepared dinner for them and did some light housecleaning. The kids' mother, Rachel, had a late night at a banquet for a charity she supported.

After dinner Blu settled the kids in with a movie. She curled up on the couch beside them and pulled out the latest book that was consuming her attention. She always made sure she had a few new ones for the summer. Even as she settled into the chapter, she found it hard to concentrate on the words.

Her mind drifted back to AJ. It had been some time since she'd last seen him, and she suspected that was why Maddie had involved him in the ice cream hunt. She loved her best friend, but Maddie had quite a tendency to think she knew what was best for Blu. She flipped to the next page in her book without having much of an idea of what had happened on the previous one. She noticed that the kids were beginning to nod off.

"Alright, time to brush your teeth. We can finish the movie in the morning."

As she helped the kids into their beds, Blu briefly forgot about AJ. But the moment that she was alone in her room, he was all she could think about.

There was something about him that she had yet to figure out. It was as if he summoned memories that she didn't even have. But the summer would come to an end soon, and so would their regular interactions. She had no interest in sparking something that would only come to an end.

As she fell asleep that night she was more determined than ever not to have anything more than a friendship with AJ.

CHAPTER 5

The next morning the children shared breakfast with Rachel. The scent of cinnamon buns and fresh coffee combined with the sound of happy voices was a great thing for Blu to wake up to.

"You should have seen the dinner last night. Duck!" Rachel scrunched up her nose and grinned at the kids. Joey gulped and Marley squeaked with disgust.

"I would never eat a duck."

"No way, you'd have to be quackers. Get it, Mom? Quackers!" Joey laughed so hard that bits of cereal flew out of his mouth.

"Oh, Joey, here." His mother handed him his napkin. "No jokes until after you're done chewing."

Blu laughed as she joined them at the table. There had been many days lately when Rachel was more sad than happy, so she was glad to see the woman smiling from ear to ear.

"It sounds like you had a good turnout for the fundraiser."

"Yes, we did. A lot of people want to develop in this area, and I'm finding they're more than happy to show that interest by donating to support local charities."

"What do you think they want to build? Hotels and such?"

"Yes—well, really anything will do well if it's on the beach. This is one of the few areas along the coast that still has so many small businesses. To be honest, I like the donations but I do hope that not too many people sell. I love coming here for the summer, mainly because it isn't as overrun with tourists as other places."

"Mr. Peddle is thinking of selling. I spoke to him yesterday about it."

"Oh wow. That would be a shame."

"Yes, it would. I don't know if I've told you this, Rachel, but I've actually been here before, and to his ice cream shop, prior to working with you, I mean."

"Oh, really? For vacation?"

"Yes. My parents weren't daring enough to take us on vacation very often, but when they did, it was usually some place nearby and cheap. Just once my father wanted to get all of us to the beach. So we came here for a couple of days one time. I ate quite a bit of ice cream during that time. I remember Mr. Peddle's shop as one of my favorite memories. I have to say I'm a little sad about the fact that he's thinking of selling."

Rachel shook her head. "These real estate investor types can be quite convincing."

"I hope that's all it is. He seemed a little intimidated."

"Hm." Rachel frowned. "Poor guy. I don't think they ever had kids. Maybe if they had someone to leave the shop to, they'd keep it open."

Blu gazed wistfully at the two children, who used their spoons to tap out a melody on their bowls. A part of her wondered if she would end up like the Peddles without any children of her own. It wasn't the worst thing that could happen. She just wasn't sure if it was what she wanted.

Later that morning Blu and the kids met up with Maddie, Brennan, and Chrissa at the park. It was a bit early still for the playground crowd, so the kids had the run of the equipment. Blu joined Maddie near the edge of the playground.

"How are you doing this morning?" Maddie yawned. "I'm having a hard time getting going today."

"Me too. I had a hard time sleeping last night."

"Oh? Anything in particular keeping you awake?"

Blu smiled at her. She knew better than to tell her the truth about what was keeping her awake.

"Too much ice cream, I guess."

"That could be it." Maddie nodded. "I can tell that I've been eating way too much sugar. I feel bad telling the kids they can't have another cookie and then holing up in my room with my own box."

"Oh, you're bad." Blu laughed. "I had an extra cup of

coffee this morning, so I should be okay."

After about twenty minutes of watching the kids play, Blu suddenly realized what that extra cup of coffee really meant.

"Oh boy, I have to get to a restroom." She cringed.

"Yup, two cups of coffee." Maddie laughed.

Blu glanced around for a restroom to use. She knew that there was one back near the ice cream shop not far from the playground.

"Maddie, would you mind keeping an eye on the kids for me while I run to the restroom?"

"No problem." Maddie picked up a football and threw it to Brennan.

Brennan watched as the football sailed right past him and into the ground.

"Did you want me to catch that?" He raised an eyebrow.

"Uh, yeah." Maddie rolled her eyes.

Blu did her best not to laugh as she hurried around the corner of the ice cream shop and walked behind it. She hurried to the restroom and took care of her bladder emergency.

As she left, she noticed something strange on the ground beside—and just a bit behind—the dumpster. It looked like a blanket. Blu was annoyed that someone would leave it on the ground instead of putting it inside the dumpster.

She walked over to it to pick it up herself. When she

drew closer she could see that it wasn't a blanket at all, but a shawl that seemed to be covering something else. Her hand trembled as she inched back the shawl to reveal Martha Peddle's face.

Blu stumbled backward until her back hit the wall of the ice cream shop. Her eyes filled with tears in the same moment that she reached for her phone. As she dialed the police she crept back to Martha's side. Though it was clear that the woman was deceased, Blu touched one hand gently as if she could still offer some comfort.

When the operator answered the phone she began to describe her location and what she'd found. A minute later sirens screamed through the balmy summer air.

Blu reluctantly stood up. She knew that Maddie and the children would look for her and she didn't want to risk them seeing Martha's body. But she couldn't bring herself to leave the woman's side.

As the first officer arrived Blu waved to get his attention.

"Over here!" Her heart beat frantically even though she knew it was already too late.

CHAPTER 6

With the police and paramedics there to take care of Martha, Blu stumbled her way out from behind the ice cream shop. She stepped into the parking lot just as Maddie and the kids approached.

"Don't go back there, Maddie. Don't." Blu tried to hide her tears but they burned her eyes. "Keep the kids away."

"What is it, Blu? Are you okay?" Maddie frowned.

"Mrs. Peddle."

"The ice cream shop owner's wife?" Maddie's eyes widened. "Is she hurt?"

"No, it's much worse." Blu turned and pulled Maddie away from the children. She lowered her voice. "She's dead, Maddie."

"What?" Maddie hugged her. "I'm so sorry."

"We shouldn't let the kids know. It will really upset them. I need to stay and speak to the police. Can you take the kids home for me?"

"Absolutely. Of course. Do you want me to keep them with me?"

"Yes, that would be good if you can. I'm not sure if Rachel is home. I'll try not to be too long."

"Okay." Maddie shook her head. "Do you think she just died of natural causes?"

"I don't know. I just assumed she did. Maybe a heart attack. I don't know."

"Try not to get too upset. Call me when you want me to bring the kids home."

"Thanks, Maddie."

Blu watched as Maddie escorted the kids to the car. She could see that Joey wanted an explanation and trusted that Maddie would no the right thing to say. Was it right to reveal something so tragic to a seven-year-old?

"Ma'am, you found the body?"

The officer's voice startled her. Only then did she recognize that she was in shock. Her senses were numbed by what she'd found and her mind struggled to process it.

"I found Mrs. Peddle, yes." Blu looked at the officer. She reached up to wipe at her eyes.

"Did you notice anything out of the ordinary on or around the body?"

"Her name is Martha. Martha Peddle." Blu stared into his eyes. "She's not a body."

"I'm sorry, ma'am, I'm just trying to get all the facts here. Can you please tell me if there was anything strange on or near the body—near Martha?"

"No. Has anyone told her husband, Gill? Gill Peddle will need to be notified right away. Oh, he's going to be heartbroken." Blu's eyes filled with hot heavy tears that her eyelashes could not hold back.

The officer cleared his throat and handed her a tissue. "Were you friends with the deceased?"

"Not exactly friends, no. But we always buy ice cream from the shop. I just hope that Gill is okay. I don't know why she would have been here all alone."

"She didn't have her purse. Did you see her purse?"

"Her purse?" Blu blinked. "No. I didn't see it. Maybe it's in the shop?"

"I don't think so. The shop is locked." The officer shook his head. "I'm sure it'll turn up somewhere."

"Do you think it was a heart attack?"

"It's possible. We won't know for sure until the autopsy is complete."

Blu shuddered at the thought. "Can I go? I really need to get back to work."

"Uh, I think Chief Pitman might want to talk to you."

Blu shook her head. The last thing she wanted was to talk to Chief Pitman. He was gruff and in her opinion quite cold. He would probably judge her for the tears she shed.

"I've given you my statement. If there's any other information you might need I'd be happy to offer it. But I'd really like to go now."

"Ma'am, I'm not sure that's a good idea."

"I'm a nanny. The family I work for is staying in a beach house nearby. I'm easy to find if you need me."

"Alright. I guess it would be okay."

"Make sure you get in contact with Gill. Okay?"

"Yes, we will."

As Blu drove out of the parking lot she could see Chief Pitman's car approaching from the other direction. She thought for just a moment about turning back. But as fresh tears built in her eyes, she couldn't bring herself to do it. She just wanted to be home, where she could pretend that nothing bad ever happened.

Blu drove to the Rosses' home where Maddie and the kids were blowing bubbles in the front yard—more specifically, Marley and Joey were blowing bubbles while Brennan and Chrissa played on their cell phones.

Maddie stood up from the front steps to greet Blu. "How did it go?"

Blu clenched her jaw and shook her head. "It's always hard for me to understand how the police are able to look at people as just bodies. I just hope that they realize they are dealing with a wonderful woman who had a big impact on the people around her."

"I'm sure that Gill will make sure they do."

"I hope so. I hate to think of how he will take this. It honestly worries me."

"He's probably stronger than you think. It will be hard for him, but he'll find a way to get through it."

"I guess." Blu smiled as Marley blew a stream of bubbles in her direction. She swatted at the bubbles playfully, even though more tears brewed. "I'd better get them home. I think once we're settled, I can start to calm down. I really appreciate you taking them for me."

"It's no problem. I hope that you can get a little rest today. Try to think of happy things. It might help to get that image out of your mind."

"It might." Blu nodded. "Alright, kiddos, let's go."

"Bye, Brennan!" Joey waved to the boy. Blu expected that Brennan wouldn't even look up from his phone, but he did.

He gave Joey a thumbs up, then went back to texting. "He's so cool!"

Blu couldn't help but smile at Joey's admiration.

CHAPTER 7

Blu drove the kids home and noticed that Rachel's car was in the driveway.

When Blu opened the door to the beach house she found Rachel on her computer in the living room.

"Blu, were you just at the playground?"

"Yes."

"Someone just sent me a message that there are a ton of police cars down there. I was about to call you to check on you guys."

"I'm sorry, I should have called to let you know that we're okay. We left when the police showed up."

"Do you know what it's about?"

Blu met her eyes. Blu had a strict policy about being honest with the parents she worked for. They trusted her with their children, and she always wanted to give them every reason to trust her.

"I'm sure that it will be on the news."

"What will be?" Rachel stood up.

"You two go wash up and I'll get you some lunch." Blu smiled at the kids.

She turned back to Rachel and was about to open her mouth to explain when there was a heavy knock at the door. Blu was relieved to answer it and halt the conversation for the moment.

"I must have forgotten something at Maddie's."

She pulled open the door to find Chief Pitman.

"Hi, Blu."

Blu frowned. "Yes. Can I help you?"

"Did you find Martha Peddle?"

Blu cleared her throat. "Yes, I did."

"Did my officer suggest that you stay at the scene until I could speak with you?" Chief Pitman leaned his shoulder against the doorframe.

"Blu, what is he talking about?" Rachel frowned. "Did you see what happened today?"

"I'd rather not talk about it." Blu tilted her head toward the two children, who had returned to the living room with a board game to set up. "It's upsetting."

"Of course it's upsetting. That's why it's so important that I get the correct information from you." Chief Pitman's voice became sharper.

"I think you need to watch your tone." Rachel moved between Blu and the chief. "There's no reason to speak to her that way."

Although Blu could see the heat ignite in Chief Pitman's eyes, she couldn't deny a hint of warmth in her heart that Rachel stood up for her.

"It's okay, Rachel. If you don't mind, I'll just speak to

him outside."

"It's fine. But if you need me just let me know." Rachel locked eyes with Chief Pitman.

He turned away and stepped outside. Blu followed after him.

"The summer people seem to think they own the law around here." Chief Pitman shook his head as he turned back to face her. "But they don't, Blu. Understand?"

"Yes, I understand. Chief Pitman, I called as soon as I saw Martha, and I stayed until help arrived. I just didn't want to upset the kids."

"You have to realize that leaving the scene of a murder was an unwise decision." He slid his hands into his pockets.

"A murder? I thought maybe she had a heart attack or something." Blu's eyes watered once more. "Who would murder her? Are you sure?"

"Yes. I'm sure."

"How?" Blu raised an eyebrow.

"When you found Martha, what did you do?"

"I don't know what you mean. I found her, and I called the police."

"No. That's not all you did. Think about it, Blu. When you found her, what did you do?"

"I told you already. I didn't do anything else. I went to the bathroom, I walked back down the alley, and I saw her."

Chief Pitman leaned toward her. His eyes bore into

hers. "What did you see?"

Blu stared back at him. Her heart skipped a beat. Her breath grew shallow. "I saw a blanket. I mean, I thought it was a blanket."

"And?"

"I was annoyed. The dumpster was right there. So I walked over to pick it up, and then I saw that it wasn't a blanket. It was a person with a shawl over her face."

"A shawl?"

"Yes."

"What did you do?"

"I called the police."

"No!" Chief Pitman's voice made her jump, not because it was loud, but because she had drifted back in her mind to the moment she found Martha. "You did something else." He searched her eyes.

"I pulled the shawl away from her face." Blu's eyes widened.

"When someone dies of natural causes, do they normally pull a shawl up over their face?"

"No." Blu closed her eyes. "No, they don't."

"No, they don't." He rested a hand on the exterior wall beside her. "So, my men spent quite some time under the assumption that this death was natural, because you never told the officer that you pulled the shawl away from Martha's face."

"I didn't even think about it. I didn't realize that it would be important." She frowned. "But you know now."

"Only because the crime scene tech found fibers of the shawl stuck in her lipstick, hair, and eyebrows. In homicide, Blu, every second counts. You need to tell me what you saw when you were there."

"I didn't see anything but Martha. I didn't witness the crime. No one else was nearby."

"Are you sure?" Chief Pitman stepped closer to her. "The medical examiner puts the estimated time of death at an hour before you discovered the body."

"An hour?" Blu's eyes widened.

"How long were you and the kids at the park?"

Blu looked away from him. A ripple of nausea washed through her. Was it possible that Mrs. Peddle was killed while they played and laughed on the playground? The very idea that the murder could have taken place right under their noses made her dizzy.

"Blu?" Chief Pitman reached out and caught her by the arm.

The gentleness of his touch caused Blu to meet his eyes. "At least an hour. Are you sure about the time of death?"

"Right now it's just an estimate. We won't know anything conclusive until the autopsy of the body is complete. If you can give me some idea of what happened, we'll have a head start on solving this crime. Anything you can think of—a strange person walking by, some kind of scream you might have heard—all of that can make a difference. So please, think about it."

"I didn't hear anything." Blu shook her head.

"See, that's what I'm having a hard time believing. You were right there. You heard nothing? Not a gasp, not a scream, no squealing tires, nothing?"

Blu stared back at him. "If I said I didn't hear anything, I didn't hear anything. Why else would I say that?"

"I don't know. I also don't know how a woman dies only a few feet away from the playground, but she doesn't make a sound. Can you see why that would not make sense to me?" He held her gaze in return.

"Yes, I can." Blu shook her head slowly. "It's heartbreaking to think that Mrs. Peddle could have been dying while we were playing on the playground. I don't know, maybe the sounds of the kids drowned out anything that came from the alley. If I knew something, Chief Pitman, I hope you know that I would tell you."

"Is it that you don't want to get involved? Usually you're chomping at the bit to help with a crime."

"Why don't you believe me?" Blu frowned. "I've never given you a reason to think that I would lie to you. So why is it that you are acting like I'm trying to cover something up?"

"Well, you certainly aren't doing much to help me. If you are so interested in solving the crime, then you should want to help. Walk me through everything that happened again."

CHAPTER 8

Blu pursed her lips and looked away from Chief Pitman. She had to admit that she was letting her aversion to him get in the way of her willingness to cooperate.

"Okay, fine. I was at the playground with the kids, my friend Maddie, and the children she takes care of. I had to use the restroom, so I walked around behind the ice cream shop to use the restroom."

"You didn't see the body on the way in?"

"I was preoccupied."

"With what?"

Blu looked at him. "What do you think?"

"I see. Then what?"

"I left the restroom and walked back down the alley. I found Mrs. Peddle. It was horrifying, and I'm sorry it happened, but I don't know anything else about it."

"Well, if your memory starts to come back, do give me a call, Blu." He nodded to her, then turned and walked away.

Rachel opened the door as soon as he was gone.

"Why didn't you tell me that you were at the scene, Blu?" She frowned.

"I just didn't want you to worry. I mean, maybe I shouldn't have stayed, but I just couldn't leave her there alone." Blu shook her head. "I didn't think that it would be right."

"I understand that. You don't ever have to hide things from me. I'm more interested in how you are doing after seeing such a terrible thing. Are you okay?"

"I think so. I just hope that they figure out who did this. Poor Martha."

"How do they think she died?"

"They're not sure yet." Blu lowered her voice. "But I did notice a strange blue tinge around her lips. I thought it was from a heart attack or something, but Chief Pitman believes it was a murder. If that's the case, then I think maybe she was suffocated."

Rachel put her hand to her mouth. "That poor woman. I would never expect something like this to happen to her."

"Me either." Blu folded her arms. "I'm really worried about Mr. Peddle."

"Well, maybe you should go see him. Take the rest of the day off. I'm sure that after what happened today, you could use it. I'm here anyway."

"Okay." Blu nodded. "That would be nice. I'm just going to check in and make sure that he has someone with him. If they had no kids, he might not."

"Good. Let me know if there's anything I can do to help. Alright?"

"Yes, I will. That's kind of you."

Blu left the house with a knot in her stomach. A part of her wanted to just walk the beach instead of checking in with Gill. She didn't want to face the truth about what happened to Martha, but it was more important to her to ensure that the man was being treated well.

As she approached the ice cream shop she walked through the parking lot of the Beach Bum. She was so focused on Martha's death that she didn't notice someone jogging across the parking lot toward her. It wasn't until he touched her on the elbow that she realized he was there.

She stopped and turned to see AJ looking at her.

"Blu, I heard that you were the one who found Martha. Are you okay?" He caught her hand.

"I'm fine. I just wanted to check in on Mr. Peddle."

"Oh." AJ looked across the parking lot at the ice cream shop. "My uncle's with him now." AJ's uncle was Chief Pitman.

"I wonder how he's taking it. That poor man. How is he going to survive without Martha?" Blu sighed. "I've never seen two people more in love."

"Blu, I think there's something that you should know."

AJ tried to get her attention by tugging at her hand, but Blu pulled it away and squinted at the ice cream shop.

She could see the door open and Chief Pitman step out, followed by several police officers and Mr. Peddle.

"Wait, what is he doing?" Blu stared at the parade of officers that surrounded Mr. Peddle as he was led out of the ice cream shop toward a patrol car.

"What he has to do." AJ placed a restraining hand on her arm. "Gill Peddle is the prime suspect."

"Mr. Peddle? But why? He would never do anything to harm his wife."

"Apparently Martha's lips were stained with blueberry."

Blu's eyes widened. "I thought they were just discolored. But why does that matter?"

"Martha had a rare but severe allergy to blueberries."

"That's why they don't carry blueberry ice cream."

AJ nodded. "It was an allergy that Gill was quite aware of, and the theory is that Gill intentionally gave his wife blueberry ice cream."

"But if she knew that she was allergic, why would she eat it?"

"They found packaging in the dumpster near the body. The ice cream container claimed it was berry cherry—a mixture of flavors, none of which were blueberry. My guess is she ate quite a bit of it before she recognized the taste, if she ever recognized it at all."

"That's horrible." Blu tried not to think about the fact that she ate the exact same flavor. "But still, that doesn't mean that Gill is at fault. Anyone could have given her the container of ice cream."

"His fingerprints were all over the container. The container was from Peddle's Ice Cream Shop. It's very simple Blu. I really don't think there's any other way it could have happened."

Blu crossed her arms. "There's no way that Gill did this."

"Listen, I've been in a police family long enough to know that when a spouse is killed, the husband or wife is always the first one they look at. In this case, there's plenty of evidence to back up the suspicion."

"Your uncle has it wrong. Gill adored Martha. They were the perfect couple. They've been together for years. They love each other. What motive could he possibly have?"

"So you know them well?" AJ titled his head toward her and lowered his voice. "You've seen them outside of the ice cream shop?"

Blu pursed her lips. "Well, no. But that doesn't mean that I'm wrong."

"And it also doesn't mean that you're right. You've got to let Uncle Paul sort it out. He's an honest man. If he thinks there's any reason to believe that someone else killed Martha, then he'll follow up on it."

CHAPTER 9

Blu tightened her arms and watched as Chief Pitman guided the fragile man into the back seat of a patrol car. "I guess it just doesn't seem fair. He just lost his wife. Now he has to go through this. How is that decent, AJ?"

"It may not be easy for him, but neither of us knows exactly what happened. It's easy to say that he did or didn't do it, but we just don't know, do we? That's why there will be an investigation."

"I want to talk to him." Blu started to walk toward the patrol car.

"No. No, I don't think that's a good idea." He pulled her back slightly.

"I can't let this happen. I can't just stand here and watch with you while he suffers in a holding cell. Or what? Is your uncle going to interrogate him?"

"Blu, take it easy." AJ met her eyes. "You have to tread carefully around my uncle."

"Maybe you have to, AJ, but I don't. I'm not going to sit by while a sweet old man is accused of such a terrible thing."

"Blu, I'm warning you."

"You don't do that." She pulled her hand firmly away from him. "You don't get to warn me. Maybe I've given you the wrong impression, AJ, but there is one thing about me that you'll learn as you get to know me. I will not stand idly by when someone is being treated unfairly."

"We're not talking about sharing toys or shoving on the playground, Blu. We're talking about interfering with a case." His forehead creased as he leaned closer to her. "I know that you're going to do what you please, but my uncle isn't the type to question. He also isn't the type to jail an innocent man."

"I guess we'll have to agree to disagree." Blu held his gaze for a long moment. "AJ, I have no intention of offending or being disrespectful to your uncle, but I will make sure that Gill is treated correctly."

AJ held his hands up in the air, nodded, and walked away. A twinge of anxiety sped up Blu's heart as she wondered if she had pushed things too far with AJ. Then she reminded herself of the promise she'd made the night before. It was better to push AJ away than to deal with the consequences of stringing him along.

As she walked across the parking lot to the ice cream shop the patrol car pulled away. She'd missed her chance to speak to Gill, but she could still take a look at the shop and the surrounding area. Most of the shop, including the area behind it that led to the bathroom, was roped off with crime scene tape. Blu's stomach fluttered again at the thought of Martha's death.

"Can I help you?" A young officer with a crisp uniform and a stern voice eyed her as she approached.

"I'm just looking."

"That's a bit morbid."

Blu offered him a faint smile. "I'm not trying to cause any trouble."

"There's no reason for you to be here, so please move along."

"Sir, I—"

"You there! Why are you taking pictures?" The officer's attention shifted to another man who stood near the police tape and was busy snapping several pictures of the ice cream shop.

Blu realized right away that he was the same man she saw walking toward the shop the day before.

The man lowered his camera. "I have every right to be here."

"You don't have a right to take photographs."

"Are you sure about that? You might want to brush up on the law."

"Are you being combative, sir? I have given you a direct order to leave the area. I suggest that you leave."

The man shifted from one foot to the other. He toyed with his camera as if he might take more pictures. Then he turned away from the officer and began to walk away.

Blu didn't wait for the officer to tell her to leave

again. Instead, she followed the man with the camera. He approached a sleek dark blue car. The license plate on the car was a vanity plate with the name STR AGNT written across the placard. He reached for the door handle of the driver's side, then paused. He spun around so fast that Blu jumped back.

"Are you following me?" He raised an eyebrow.

Blu studied his business suit and suitcase. She was sure he was the same man from the day before.

"What business do you have with Gill Peddle?"

He turned all the way around and leaned back against his spotless car. "And you are?"

"My name is Blu."

"Blu?" He smiled a little. "Interesting. So why are you following me?"

"A woman was murdered, and I want to know how you are involved."

"How am I involved in a murder? I'm not. That's absurd. I'm here on a professional basis."

"Oh? Snapping pictures of crime scenes is your job?"

He cleared his throat. "Snapping pictures of real estate that I have an interest in is. I need to ensure that my client has up-to-date photographs of the land he intends to purchase."

"So you're the real estate agent that has been pressuring Mr. Peddle?"

"I do my job—if that's what you mean. Still, you haven't told me what your interest in all of this is?"

"I'm a friend of Mr. Peddle's."

"Are you? Then I'm sure you knew his wife, and I'm sorry for your loss. However, I'm not a friend, and I do not care if ten people were murdered, I only care about my client's interests. Now that I know a murder has been committed on this property, that should help me in future negotiations."

"You are heartless." Blu narrowed her eyes.

"I didn't get to where I am by being kind. I don't care what people think of me." He shrugged. "Least of all a random woman that stalks people."

"I wasn't stalking you."

"Sure." He turned back to his car and opened the door.

"Wait. What's your name?" Blu stepped closer to him.

"Why would you want to know the name of a heartless man?"

"I'm just curious." Blu offered him a feigned sweet smile.

"It's Ken Buchman."

"Wonderful, Ken Buchman. You should know that if I see you harassing Gill or loitering around his property I will file a complaint with the local police."

"Oh?" He smirked. "Good luck with that." He pulled open the car door and got in, then slammed it closed again.

CHAPTER 10

Blu watched as Ken Buchman drove out of the parking lot. She hadn't mentioned seeing him the day before to Chief Pitman, but now she wished that she had.

As she headed back to the beach house she dialed Maddie's phone number.

"What's happening, Blu? Are you okay?"

"I'm fine. I'm sorry about today. I lost it."

"Of course you did. After what you saw how could you not?"

"I don't know what to think, Maddie. They just took Mr. Peddle to the police station."

"Are you serious? They really think he had something to do with it?"

"It certainly looks that way. I think I might need your help."

"With what? You know I'll do anything."

"Rachel mentioned that she didn't think Mr. Peddle had any kids. He may not have many living relatives. I'm just worried that he won't have anybody to stand up for him. As devastated as he must be with the loss of his wife, I hate to think of him going through all of this alone. I'm going to take a ride down to the police station and check on him."

"Oh, I bet Chief Pitman will just love that."

"Well, I have something else I want to tell him. Hopefully that will make him more responsive."

"Maybe. But watch yourself, Blu; you don't want to get into anything that you can't get out of, that's for sure. In the meantime I'll check into Mr. Peddle and see if he has any family we might not know about. He might be too grief-stricken to even notify them."

"Good idea. Thanks so much, Maddie."

"Any time."

"You're the best. I don't know what I'd do without you here. You've really been helping me out a lot lately."

"Well, you've certainly helped me out in the past. It's the least I can do," said Maddie.

Blu hung up the phone as she reached the driveway to the beach house. She got behind the wheel of her car and drove to the police station. Her swirling thoughts focused in on the last few times she'd seen Martha. The confrontation at the mall suddenly came to the forefront of her mind.

She parked her car in the parking lot of the police station and took a minute to try to remember exactly what was said between the two women.

When she walked into the police station there was quite a bit of activity—phones were ringing, uniformed police officers hurried in and out of the restricted section. Blu caught sight of Chief Pitman just as he was about to disappear down a hallway.

"Chief Pitman!" She rushed forward. "Chief Pitman!"

He paused and looked over at her. His nostrils flared and his upper lip curled.

"What is it, Blu?"

"I need to speak to you for a moment."

"I'm a little busy right now—solving crime, protecting the city, and so forth."

"I understand, but I think you're going to want to hear what I have to say. Please, can I have just a minute of your time?" Blu offered her most endearing smile.

Chief Pitman sighed so heavily that his shoulders slumped. "Alright, one minute. That's it."

"Great." Blu walked toward him.

One of the uniformed officers tried to step in front of her. "Wait a minute, you can't go back there."

"It's okay, just let her go. Nothing can stop this one." Chief Pitman rolled his eyes.

Blu smiled a little at what she took as a compliment about her determination.

"Chief, how could you arrest Gill?"

"Oh? This is what you needed my time for? To question my skills as a law enforcement officer? Are you aware that they don't just hand out these chief of police titles? They actually have to be earned through education and experience, not to mention the confidence of an entire community and police force."

"Alright, alright. I'm sorry. But I know that Gill didn't do this. He has to be beside himself with worry."

"Oh, you know that, do you?" He met her eyes. "Then why do you think Gill just finished giving me his confession?"

"What?" Blu's eyes widened.

"Surprised?"

"Very. Are you sure that he did it?"

"Well people don't usually fess up to murder on a whim."

"But Chief, there are other suspects. Just today when I was near the ice cream shop, I saw this man trying to take pictures."

"Oh, I know about him."

"Yes, well, I saw the same man yesterday walking toward the ice cream shop, so that means that he was likely scoping the place out—maybe even stalking Martha."

"Is that what you think?" Chief Pitman shook his head. "Well, there you go—let's throw out the confession and arrest the real estate agent for doing his job."

"But Chief, he has this terrible attitude—"

"If attitudes were the issue, half of this city would be in jail. Listen, Blu, I do appreciate your enthusiasm, but at some point you're going to have to realize that you're not a police officer. I, along with my very talented employees, can handle the crime in this town."

"Okay. Then how about the woman who had a screaming match with Mrs. Peddle at the mall yesterday?"

"Huh? What woman?"

Blu couldn't help feeling a little smug in reaction to the curiosity in his voice. "I saw Martha at the mall yesterday. I was going to say hello, but she was in the middle of an argument with another woman and so I decided to stay out of it. But I did see her and the other woman."

"What were they arguing about?"

"I'm not sure. The other woman said something like 'He's a liar, you both are.' I honestly don't remember if that's exactly what she said, but it was something like that."

"Did Martha mention the other woman's name, or maybe what she was accusing her of?"

"No. That's all I heard. But the other woman was angry. I can tell you that much."

"Well, that's not much, Blu. I appreciate the intel, but I don't think it's going to lead us anywhere. In fact it sounds more like this incident might have been the tragic consequence of a lover's triangle."

"What?" Blu shook her head. "That's crazy. Martha and Gill were in love. There's no way he would ever do anything to jeopardize that."

"According to Gill, he had something to do with his wife's death. Now, if you'd like to argue with the man, feel free. But as far as I'm concerned if he wants to confess to murdering his wife, that's his business."

"Even if it's a lie?" Blu met his eyes directly.

Chief Pitman stared at her for a moment, then he sighed. "If you can find me something solid that points to anyone else, then let me know. Until then, you need to let me get my work done and stay out of it."

"Thanks a lot, Chief Pitman." Blu pursed her lips. "Can I see him? Mr. Peddle?"

"No. He's in custody. If you want to see him you'll have to go through his lawyer. But he's going to have to hire one first. Good day, Blu." He turned and walked away from her.

This time when Blu tried to follow after him, the officer put a restraining hand on her shoulder. "You can't go back there."

"Fine." Blu nodded. "Fine."

She hurried back to her car, more determined than ever to get to the truth.

CHAPTER 11

Blu tried to be quiet when she opened the door to the beach house, but Rachel was waiting for her in the living room.

"Blu? Did you find out anything?"

Blu sighed as she walked over to the couch. "Nothing good."

"What do you mean?"

"They've arrested Gill. They think that he's the one who killed Martha."

"Oh, that's terrible. Why would he do such a thing?"

"I don't think he did."

"Do the police have any other suspects?" Rachel slid over on the couch so that Blu could sit beside her.

"Even if they did, they won't follow up on them."

"Huh? Why not?"

"Because Gill confessed."

Rachel grimaced. "How awful. So he did do it then?"

"I really don't think so, Rachel. I know that a confession is pretty damning, but I really don't think it was him. I think he's devastated by Martha's death and not thinking straight. I know he has a lot of respect for Chief Pitman, and maybe he's intimidated by him."

"You think the chief forced a confession?"

"I think he might have taken advantage of Gill's grief and put more pressure on him than he should have. Gill's all alone in there. He has no one to stand up for him and protect him. Rachel?" She looked into the woman's eyes. "Remember when you asked me to let you know if he needed anything?"

"Yes."

"I think he needs a lawyer—a good one. Not the one the city has to provide to him. I know it's a lot to ask, but do you think one of your connections might be able to help him? Or maybe you could help him?"

Rachel frowned and leaned back against the couch. "Yes, that's a lot—not just because of the money, but with the crime he's accused of that could damage our family name."

"But he's innocent, Rachel, I know he is."

"I'd have to talk to Marshall about it."

"I understand that, and I respect that. But I'm not sure that Mr. Peddle has that kind of time. He has no one to help him."

"Blu, why are you so sure that he didn't do this?'

"He loved her—a real, lifetime-long love. It's tragic enough that it ends in murder—it's even worse if it ends like this."

"I'll call Marshall now. If he okays it, then we'll get the ball rolling. Okay?" She squeezed Blu's hand.

"Thank you, Rachel. I think I'm going to go freshen up."

"Take it easy, Blu, it's been a wild day."

Blu stepped into her room and shut the door. She leaned her back against it as she closed her eyes. The moment her eyes were closed she was in the alley again. Her heart ached for Martha and for Gill. She wanted to believe that Chief Pitman was as honest as AJ claimed, but she wasn't sure. After all, he had accepted the confession of an innocent man.

With the weight of his instruction to find a better suspect weighing on her mind, she headed for the shower. Aside from running, a hot shower was the best way to clear her mind. The white noise of the water, as it engulfed her, inspired a sense of relaxation that allowed her mind to quiet.

No matter what she might have thought about the chief, he did point out the mistakes she'd made when she found Martha—things she barely remembered. He also shot down the only other suspects that she was able to come up with.

She turned the water off and stepped out of the shower. Once she was dry, she dressed in a comfortable pair of pants and loose top. Then she pulled two photo albums off her shelf. Before she opened them she called

Maddie.

"Hello?"

"Hi, Maddie. Did you find anything?"

"Unfortunately not. If there are any family members, I can't find them. I mean there are plenty of Peddles out there, but I haven't been able to connect them. I'm sorry, Blu."

"Don't be. You tried."

"How is Gill?"

"I didn't actually get to see him. I think I've hit a dead end when I've barely even started. Do you want to come over for a bit?"

"I'd love to. Penelope is taking the kids out tonight, so I'm free. I can be there in ten minutes."

"Awesome. Thanks for the company, Maddie."

She hung up the phone and set the albums aside to look through with Maddie. When she walked out into the living room to wait for her, Rachel met her there.

"I spoke with Marshall. He agreed to use our connections, but none of this can come back on us. So we're going to send a friend of ours to look over the case and speak to Gill. If he decides that there's a chance that Gill is innocent, he'll take the case. I'm sorry. I know that's not exactly what you wanted, but it's the best that we can do."

"No, that's wonderful. It's more than I could have hoped for, Rachel, and I'm sure that Gill will be grateful for it."

"I'll go ahead and make the call then." As Rachel walked off there was a knock on the door.

Blu braced herself when she opened it, just in case it was another visit from Chief Pitman. To her relief, it was Maddie holding out a two fresh cups of coffee.

"Oh, thank you!" Blu took one of the cups and led Maddie back to her room.

CHAPTER 12

As Blu and Maddie settled in, she filled her friend in on the latest about the case. "So there's not much to do now but wait. I need something to take my mind off of Gill being in that holding cell. I thought I'd look through the pictures from our visits to the ice cream shop and pick out a few. I think we should create a memory memorial for Martha. I'm sure other people in the community will have some to contribute."

"That's a sweet idea." Maddie picked up the other album and began looking through it.

Blu flipped through the summer scrapbook that she and the kids had made the year before. It was filled with memories of all the fun activities that they'd done. Just as she expected, there was a full page for ice cream day. In the photograph the kids and the Peddles stood in front of the ice cream shop. Marley, much tinier and still quite shy, gripped her big brother's hand tight. Joey gazed up at Mr. Peddle with a wide smile and cheeks smeared with ice cream. The Peddles had their arms locked together. It was a picture-perfect moment that warmed Blu's heart.

"Look at that love. That's not something that ends in murder."

Maddie leaned over her shoulder to look at the photograph. "It's a beautiful picture. You should use that if we put together a memorial. Too bad that guy photo-bombed it."

"Huh?" Blu squinted her eyes.

"Here, in the window." Maddie tapped the portion of the photograph with the large front window of the ice cream shop.

Clearly reflected in the window was a man holding a camera. It wasn't a digital camera, or a cell phone camera. It looked like a camera that still used film. Blu had never noticed the reflection before, as it was off-center. Her focus was always on the children. The reflection made the man look as if he might have stood directly behind Blu.

How had she not noticed him there? More importantly, why was he taking a photograph of the Peddles and the kids? The thought of some strange man out there with the same picture left her feeling very unsettled.

"I never noticed that before. That's odd, isn't it?"

"A bit."

"Why would he be taking a picture of the kids?"

Maddie tilted the scrapbook a little. "You know I love taking pictures. I'm pretty sure from the way his camera is tilted that he wasn't taking a picture of the kids. It seems like maybe he was either taking a picture of the Peddles or something that was above their heads."

"What would be above their heads?" The photograph cut off the top of the shop door.

"Maybe if you go take a look you'll notice something."

Blu nodded. "I think that's a good idea."

"And maybe while you're there, you can ask AJ if he'll host the memorial wall at the Beach Bum."

"AJ again?" Blu raised an eyebrow. "I'm starting to think you have a crush on him, Maddie."

"Well, I need a backup plan in case the Alexander Dreamy plan fails." Maddie laughed at her joke.

"Good point." Blu smiled. "I have the rest of the evening off, so I should have plenty of time to figure it out."

"Unfortunately I don't. I've got some serious housekeeping to catch up on."

"That's okay." Blu eyed her for a moment. "This isn't some plot to get me and AJ alone, is it?"

"Would it work?"

"To be honest, I think it's best if it doesn't."

"Really?"

"Summers come to an end, right?"

"Yes, that's true. Well then, I'll stop pestering you, I promise." She winked. "Let me know how things turn out."

"I will."

After Maddie left, Blu set the books back on the

shelf. Then she changed into more presentable clothing.

She drove back to the ice cream shop and parked. She walked across the parking lot to the Beach Bum. When she stuck her head through the door she could see that the bar was crowded.

She noticed one of the waitresses.

"Is AJ here?"

"No. If you see him tell him to get back to work, we're very busy."

"Will do."

Blu ducked back out of the bar. She walked back across the parking lot to the ice cream shop. It was still roped off, but there weren't any police present. Blu stared up at the roof. All she saw was a roof. She didn't notice anything particularly special about it.

She took a few steps back in an attempt to position herself exactly where she thought the man from the photo would have been standing. When she lifted her eyes to the roof again, she noticed a shimmer. The last of the evening light seemed to be bouncing off something up there. It held her attention. She took another slight step back and tilted her head in an attempt to see even further. When she did, her back struck something solid.

CHAPTER 13

"Blu, what are you doing?"

She spun around to see AJ behind her.

"Oh, I'm sorry, I didn't see you there."

He raised an eyebrow. "I was behind you. I'm sorry I didn't move out of your way."

They stood so close that the tension between them seemed to fill the space. "I was looking for you," said Blu.

"Oh?" His casual smile helped her to relax. "I don't spend much time on the roof."

"Always sarcastic." Blu rolled her eyes. "I was looking for you at the bar, but you weren't there."

"Yes, I was occupied with something. You can always call me, you know."

"Well, the question I wanted to ask is a bit too sensitive for a phone call. And also, your waitress is missing you."

"Sensitive?" His eyes widened a little. "Are you finally going to say yes to dinner with me?"

"I don't remember you asking." She tilted her head to the side.

"Oh, you should." He grinned.

Blu almost mirrored his expression, then she remembered why she wanted to talk to him.

"I thought it would be nice to have a memorial wall for Martha where people could post pictures of their memories at the ice cream shop, and I was hoping that you would agree to host it."

"Ah. That kind of sensitive." He ran his palm along the back of his neck. "I don't know, Blu. I'd have to run it by my uncle."

Blu lifted an eyebrow. "You have to get his permission?"

"Of course not." He shoved his hands into his pockets. "It's a matter of respect. The case is still active."

"Oh, does he consider it active? I thought he got his man." Blu crossed her arms.

AJ met her eyes, his lips half-turned up and his lashes narrowed. "I guess you don't agree."

"You know I don't. Gill wouldn't do that to his wife."

"So you say. But my uncle sees things differently at the moment. I don't want to step on his toes. I'll check with him, and as long as he is fine with it, I'll host it."

Blu pursed her lips. It was not exactly the answer that she wanted, but she could tell from the tension of AJ's shoulders and the set of his jaw that it was the only one she was going to get.

She glanced away from him, back up at the roof. When she did, a flash of light caught her right in the eyes.

She winced and drew back, which caused her to collide with AJ once more. He instinctively swept an arm around her waist to steady her.

"What is that?" Blu squinted.

"What?"

"There's something shiny on the roof."

"Maybe a rusted shingle, or something that got stuck up there."

"Hm." Blu studied the slope of the roof. "Is there a way to get up there?"

"A way to get on the roof of a building that doesn't belong to you and that you have no reason to be climbing? Oh, let's not forget, it's part of a murder investigation."

"The murder took place in the alley."

"Actually the death took place in the alley, but Martha could have eaten the ice cream anywhere."

"Are you sure you're not the cop in the family?" Blu rolled her eyes and strolled right past him. Before he could stop her she grabbed a ladder from behind the ice cream shop. She positioned it at what she thought would be an easy access point.

"Blu."

She put one foot on the bottom rung.

"Blu, I don't think this is a good idea."

"Still doing it." She climbed up to the next rung.

"Alright, alright. Here, let me get that." He grabbed the ladder and held it steady.

As Blu climbed higher she could see a metal object on the roof. She couldn't figure out what it was. "I'm going onto the roof."

"Blu, don't! You might fall."

"I'm not going to fall. I'll be just fine." She climbed up onto the roof and promptly slid right down to her knees. "Ouch."

"Blu!" AJ surged up the ladder to help her, but she waved him away.

"I'm fine, I promise. Just give me a second."

She edged her way along the roof. Its sharp slope made it difficult to keep her balance. When she reached the metal object she discovered that it was a large horseshoe.

"Hurry up, someone's coming."

Blu grabbed the horseshoe and gave it a hard tug. It wouldn't budge. This wasn't just something that had been placed on the roof; it was anchored to the roof. She wondered why anyone would affix the horseshoe to the roof in a place where no one could see it. She gave up on getting it free and inched her way back to the ladder. Before she made it all the way there, voices drifted up to her.

"Hey, Uncle Paul."

"AJ, what are you doing?"

"Uh. I noticed that there was some damage on the roof. I was just going to snap a picture of it. I thought maybe it was from that last storm that rolled through."

"Why would you think that was a good idea?"

"You know me, always keeping myself busy."

"Really? Because I got a call from one of your waitresses wanting to make a missing persons report on you."

"I was just headed over."

Blu held her breath and flattened herself against the slope of the roof. The last thing she needed was to have to explain herself to Chief Pitman.

"So what kind of damage did you find?"

"Not much—just a little wind damage."

"What's going on, AJ?" Chief Pitman's voice hardened. "Are you hiding something from me?"

"No, sir."

Blu bit into her bottom lip. Despite AJ's being about the same age as her, and much larger than Chief Pitman, she could hear the deference in his voice.

"I know you, AJ. I know when you're lying to me. You had better think long and hard about whether it's worth being deceitful."

"It's nothing, Uncle Paul. I swear."

"It better be. Do you want some help with the ladder?"

"No, I'll get it."

"Alright. I came by looking for that nanny. Blu, right?"

"You know her name, Uncle Paul."

"Right. Well, if you see her, let me know. I want to

speak to her."

"About what?"

"If you're going to keep secrets, AJ, then so am I. Just tell me if you see her."

CHAPTER 14

Blu heard his footsteps as he walked away. She knew that if she did anything to draw Chief Pitman's attention he'd spot her and know that AJ was lying through his teeth. She also wondered what he wanted to speak to her about. Her statement had already been given.

Just when she thought she might be in the clear, Chief Pitman stopped and turned back to look at AJ. Blu held her breath. All it would take was one look up and the chief would see that she was there. That would be it. She couldn't begin to imagine how angry he would be at AJ.

"I mean it, AJ. If you see her, I want to know. You might be sweet on her, but she has information about my case."

"Yes, sir." AJ nodded.

Chief Pitman turned and walked around the building back to his car.

Blu waited to hear the engine start, then fade away. Only then did she inch her way back to the ladder. AJ held it steady as she climbed back down.

"What was that about?"

"He seems to want to speak to you."

"Hm." Blu met his eyes. "Thanks for not telling him I was here."

"I couldn't think of a good way to explain it, considering that I don't have a clue what you were even doing up there."

"Well, I found what was shiny."

"What is it?"

"A horseshoe. I couldn't get it free."

"What do you think it means?"

"I'm not sure. But I think it's there for a reason. Someone went to a lot of trouble to put it there."

"People have weird tastes in decoration sometimes."

"That's true, but why place something as a decoration that no one else can see?"

"It's possible that Gill didn't even know it was there." AJ shrugged. "Things happen."

"I guess I'd better see what your uncle wanted."

"He's not going to stop looking for you until you do. Remember, Blu, he's trying to solve the murder too."

"And I am just trying to help." Blu winked at him. "Let me know about the memorial wall."

"I will."

Blu left the ice cream shop and drove toward the police station. She was tempted to go back to the beach house instead, but she did want to cooperate with Chief Pitman. If there was something that he needed from her, she wanted to be able to provide it.

When she walked into the police station she found Chief Pitman right away. He sat just behind the front desk at a smaller desk. His gaze was focused on something he had right in front of him.

"I heard that you were looking for me."

"Ah, the elusive Nanny Blu." He folded his hands over the soft mound of his stomach.

"It's just Blu."

"Alright. Sit." He gestured to the chair opposite him.

Blu sat down and looked up at him. "What is this about?"

"I feel like you and I have the wrong idea about one another."

"Oh?"

"When I asked for your cooperation, I meant it." He sat forward in his chair and met her eyes. "You might not be a police officer, but you do seem to have a nose for things. When I say I want your help, I mean it."

Blu blinked. She furrowed an eyebrow. "Are you joking?"

"No. I'm not." He grimaced. "I am not the most likable man, I know that. But I am also not the person that you think I am."

"I don't know you, Chief Pitman. I try to reserve judgment."

Chief Pitman quirked his lip. "Well, I know some things about you. Your lawyer showed up."

"He's not my lawyer."

"You're right, he's Gill's lawyer. But it was your influence that brought him here. I know that. I respect that."

"Why the sudden change of heart? I thought that you were convinced that Gill was the killer?"

"I'm still suspicious of him, but I've discovered a few things about Gill. He seems to be carrying a very heavy burden of guilt that goes beyond Martha's death. I feel like he's keeping something from me. No matter what you may believe, Blu, I'm not interested in just closing a case. I want to know that the right person is paying for the crime. The last thing I would ever want is to see an innocent person behind bars. If you don't know that about me, then I've given you the wrong impression."

Blu experienced some relief at his strong stance. It gave her some comfort to think that she and Chief Pitman really were working on the same side.

"If there's any way I can help, then yes, I'd like to. I'm just not sure what more I can offer."

"Well, so far you've brought me more information than anyone else involved in the investigation. You're also my one and only witness."

"But I didn't witness anything. We've been over this already."

"You were near the scene of the crime the day before the murder, and very likely during the murder. Although you may not be able to remember, I believe you heard and saw more than you realize."

"Well, if anything comes up, I'll be sure to let you know."

"I was wondering if you would do a walk-through with me. Back through the scene. Say, first thing in the morning?"

"I don't know. I'll have the kids."

"AJ can keep an eye on them."

"Okay, if he doesn't mind."

"He won't."

"Then I'll see you in the morning."

He held his hand out to her. "Thanks for coming in, Blu."

Blu gave his hand a quick shake. "Does this mean that I can see Gill?"

"Not tonight. Maybe after our walk-through tomorrow. I look forward to working with you, Blu."

Blu studied him for a moment. She wasn't sure whether to be convinced of his change of heart, but his expression gave her no reason to doubt him.

"See you then."

As she left the police station her mind wandered back to the horseshoe. She was sure that it meant something. She made a mental note to speak with Gill about it the next day.

CHAPTER 15

That night Blu spent some time talking to Maddie on the phone about her exploration of the roof.

"I really think that the horseshoe means something. If the man in the photograph was so intent on taking the picture, he had to have known that it was there."

"Especially with that old-fashioned camera. Even two years ago, not many people were still taking pictures with film."

"Hm. I wonder."

"What?"

"Well, maybe if he got the pictures developed in the area we could figure out who it is somehow."

"That's a good idea. I think the only place that still develops in town is Power's Pharmacy. Otherwise he would have had to go a little ways out of town."

"Alright, I'll check it out tomorrow." Blu yawned. "Wow, it's been a long day."

"Yes, it has. Good night, Blu."

"Good night, Maddie."

Blu curled up in her bed and tried to sleep. The more

she tried to sleep the more she thought about the case. It was exciting to think that Chief Pitman was really going to allow her to be openly involved in the investigation. That would make things a lot easier than trying to sneak around behind his back.

As she drifted off to sleep her thoughts were on horseshoes.

The next morning Blu woke up early and prepared a hearty breakfast for the kids. Rachel was already gone for the morning, as she had a meeting with the organizers of the end-of-summer blast—a party that just about everyone that owned a beach house was involved in.

Blu settled a war between the children after breakfast. She washed the dishes, made sure the kids were dressed, and then sent a text to Maddie.

Wish me luck today with Chief Pitman.

A moment later Maddie texted her back.

Good luck. I'm going to do some digging of my own.

Blu wasn't sure what Maddie meant by that, but there wasn't enough time to find out. She had to get to the ice cream shop to meet up with Chief Pitman.

On the drive she looked in the rearview mirror at the children.

"How would you two like to spend some time playing with AJ this morning?"

"Yes!" Joey rocked back and forth. "He is so much fun!"

"Beach Bum!" Marley grinned.

"Yes, well he might prefer to be called AJ, Marley." Blu grinned into the mirror.

She parked near the ice cream shop. Right away she noticed AJ's jeep in the parking lot. He stood beside it and watched as they piled out of the car. Blu tensed a little at the thought of leaving the kids with him, not because she didn't trust him, but because it was her job to look after them."

"Are you sure that you're up for this, AJ?"

"Always. I love hanging out with these two. I have just one question." His expression grew serious.

"What is it?" Joey looked up at him.

"Who is ready to bury me in the sand?"

"Me! Me!" Marley barreled toward him.

"Is your uncle here yet?" Blu scanned the parking lot.

"He's running a few minutes behind, but he'll be here."

"I'll walk down to the beach with you for a few minutes, then."

She followed the eager kids, who ran toward the sand. As it was still early, the beach was fairly empty.

"Look, a clue!" Marley pointed to the shoe she'd found two days before.

"No, Marley. That's not a clue. Remember? It's just a smelly old shoe. I guess nobody is going to come back for it." Blu picked it up off the ground. As she did, she heard a car pull into the parking lot behind her.

She turned back to see that it was Chief Pitman's car.

"Oops, I'd better go meet him."

"We'll be right here when you're done." AJ waved to her.

CHAPTER 16

Blu carried the shoe with her with the intention of throwing it in the garbage. As she walked up to Chief Pitman she wondered for a moment if she should tell him about the horseshoe.

"Just give me a second. I want to throw this out." Blu held up the shoe.

"I'll walk with you." He fell into step beside her. "Where did you find that worn-out thing?"

"Oh, it was on the beach. Actually Marley found it two days ago, but we left it there in case someone came back for it. It was still there this morning, so I thought it was time to throw it away."

"Hm. Can I see it?" He reached for the shoe.

"Sure."

"Look at this." He pointed out purplish staining on the sole of the shoe and around the toe.

"I don't know. It looks a bit like marker. But these shoes look like they would belong to a grown man," said Blu.

"Interesting." He turned the shoe over in his hand. "Blu, I'm starting to think that you're my good luck charm."

"Is that so?" She smiled. "Why is that?"

"Because I don't think that's marker on this shoe. I think it's blueberry. I'll have to have it tested at the lab of course, but I'm pretty certain that's what it is."

Blu stared at the shoe. Marley's sweet voice rang out in her mind. She called it a clue twice and Blu had been clueless.

"Wow, I can't believe I almost threw it out."

"You said you couldn't find the other shoe?"

"We didn't see it anywhere on the beach during our hunt."

"Okay. Why would someone leave one shoe on the beach?"

"I don't know." Blu shook her head. "It doesn't make much sense—just like the rest of this case."

"Well, I hope that you can help me with that. It's your insight that I think will make a difference."

"I'm not sure how I can help, but I'll certainly try."

"First, take a deep breath. I mean, a real deep down in the bottom of your belly breath."

Blu did as he instructed. For the first time since she found Martha's body she began to relax. "Okay."

"Now, just think back to the playground. The kids are playing…what are you doing?"

"Talking to Maddie."

"Okay. Anything in particular?"

Blu caught herself before she mentioned AJ. "Not really—just talking. Then I had to use the restroom, so I asked Maddie to keep an eye on the kids. I walked back here to use the restroom. I didn't see anything unusual in the alley on the way in."

"So, do you think Martha wasn't there at that time?"

"No. It wasn't that. It was the angle. When I came back out of the restroom I could see her, whereas when I'd gone in, she was sort of behind the dumpster and not visible when I was walking the other way."

"Okay." Chief Pitman walked over to the dumpster. "So, she might have been standing here." He angled himself slightly behind the dumpster.

"Yes."

"What does that look like to you?"

"What do you mean?"

"I mean, does it look like someone who was enjoying ice cream, or does it look like someone who was trying to hide? Why in this whole alley would she be ducked behind the dumpster?"

"Was there any evidence of her being moved?"

"No. There were no drag marks. Her clothes were in place. I don't think that she was moved. I think this is where she passed out."

"Okay, then she was hiding."

"But why?" Chief Pitman shook his head. "She owned the shop, she could have been inside it. She knew plenty of people in the area. She could have even been down at the beach. Why was she behind this dumpster?"

Blu frowned. She walked around behind the dumpster. "I don't see anything strange."

"It's been well searched. We even took soil samples."

"No footprints?"

"Sand and pavement don't offer much."

"So, we know that she didn't make the ice cream herself. Someone gave it to her, with her not suspecting that it contained the very thing she was deathly allergic to. We know that she would have passed out pretty quickly after ingesting it. That means she was likely here eating her ice cream."

"She threw the container out in the dumpster."

"Or did she?" Blu crouched down low beside the dumpster. "Did you see this?"

Chief Pitman looked at the spot on the side of the dumpster that Blu pointed to. There were tiny flecks of ice cream.

"No, we must have missed that." He pulled out his phone to snap a picture and then send it with a text. "I'll get my guys to get a sample and confirm it's the same ice cream."

Blu was thoughtful as she worked to get a picture of what might have happened in her head. "She's eating her ice cream—here behind the dumpster. She passes out, falls to the ground, and the cup hits the ground—which caused some of the ice cream to splatter up against the side of the dumpster."

"Yes, that makes sense." Chief Pitman nodded. "We already know that someone put the shawl over her face. Now we also know that someone threw that cup into the dumpster."

"Someone took the time to cover her face and throw out the cup." Blu shook her head. "This is so clearly a frame."

"What do you mean?"

"If you were Gill and you wanted to kill your wife, would you make her blueberry ice cream in a cup from your shop? Would you give her that ice cream at your shop? Would you then throw the cup out in the dumpster to be found? Clearly someone wanted us to point the finger at Gill."

"I have to say that I agree with you, Blu. But that still doesn't explain why Gill would confess."

"That's why I'm looking forward to speaking with him. I'd like to do that now, if that's okay?"

"Yes, that's fine. We need to clear the scene. I'm going to have this whole area processed again."

"That sounds like a good idea. Maybe they'll find some trace evidence of who might have been here with Martha."

"Maybe. I'll drive you over to the station if you'd like."

"I have the kids, remember? I can't leave them with AJ for that long."

"I'll meet you there. I'll give the little ones a tour of the station while you talk with Gill. I'm hoping that you can get something more from him. I want to know what he knows."

"Me too." Blu frowned. "I'll meet you there."

CHAPTER 17

Blu walked back to the beach, where the squeals of the children's laughter alerted her to their location before she'd had the chance to spot them. She could see Marley and Joey, but she didn't see AJ anywhere.

"AJ?" She walked up to the kids.

"Help, please don't step on me." AJ laughed as he looked up at her from a mound of sand that was piled on top of him. "They take this burying thing very seriously."

"I see that." Blu laughed. "Oh, the things I could get away with right now." She grinned.

"Don't even think about it!"

"Fine." She sighed dramatically. "Let's see who can unbury AJ the fastest."

The kids went to work digging away the sand that they'd piled on top of him. Once AJ was free, he stood up and brushed off his chest.

Blu did her best not to notice the rippling of his skin as his chest muscles shifted.

"How did the walk-through go?"

"We found a few things. Your uncle said that I can speak with Gill at the station."

"Oh, well, I can keep the kids a bit longer."

"No, that's okay. I'll bring them with me. He offered to give them a tour."

"See." AJ grinned. "All bark, no bite."

"But still plenty of bark."

"You'll get used to it."

AJ walked Blu and the kids to the car.

"Well, it won't be too much longer. Summer comes to an end, you know," said Blu.

AJ met her eyes across the top of the car. "It does. But I assume you'd be back next year?"

Blu made sure the kids' car doors were closed before she answered. "I hope to be, but with a job as a nanny you never know what might happen. The family might want a change, they might decide against a nanny, or I might be offered a better position."

"Ah." He nodded. "That doesn't mean you couldn't come back."

Blu smiled at him as she climbed into the car.

AJ lingered a moment, then walked away.

Blu started the car.

"Alright, you two have to be on your best behavior because we're going to a police station!"

Blu couldn't help but wonder what kind of stories they would tell their mother about their day. If she wasn't careful she might really be looking for a new position.

At the police station the activity was just as amplified as it had been the day before. Blu could see that Chief Pitman was using all of his resources to investigate the case.

"There they are! My junior deputies!" Chief Pitman walked over to the kids. "Ready for the grand tour?"

"Yes, please." Joey beamed.

"Blu, you can go right in—third door on your left. See if you can get him to talk to you. He's not telling me anything."

Blu nodded.

When she stepped inside the room she was stunned by how thin and small Gill looked. He was dwarfed by the long wooden table he sat at.

"Hi, Blu."

"Hi, Mr. Peddle." She sat down across from him.

"Please, call me Gill. After all, you've gone to so much trouble to help me." He frowned.

"That's because I don't think you did this. I don't understand why you keep claiming that you did."

"It's not something that you need to understand, Blu. I appreciate your support, but it's terribly misguided."

"I don't believe that." Blu met his eyes across the table. "I'm not sure why you can't tell me the truth, but I will find out."

"Blu, please."

"What about the horseshoe on the roof of the store,

Gill? Why did you put that there?" At the same time that Blu was asking the question about the roof, she saw a small part of a tattoo on Gill's arm that she'd never noticed before. The part that wasn't covered up by his sleeve looked like two ends of a horseshoe.

He laughed a little. "Oh, that." He shrugged. "It's just for luck—to bring in good steady business. Martha and I put it there on a lark."

"But why did you hide it?"

"I didn't want people to get the wrong impression and think that we were superstitious. It was just something that we did as a little tradition for ourselves. We didn't think that anyone else needed to see it."

"I see." Blu studied him. "Did you really mix blueberries into ice cream and serve it to your wife, Gill? Is that what you're telling me?"

Gill closed his eyes.

Blu could see the pain in his face as the lines in his cheeks and around his eyes deepened.

"I don't have anything to say to you about that."

"Okay." Blu frowned. "Then is there anything that you need? Anything that I can bring you?"

"I could use a book. And my shoes. They brought me in with my work shoes on and they're a bit tight on me. My old pair of shoes would be nice. Thank you."

"I'll get those for you. Is there anyone I can contact for you? Family? Friends?"

Gill's expression darkened. "Martha and I kept to

ourselves. We got used to that lifestyle. So no, I don't think there would be anyone to contact. That makes your effort all the more valuable to me, Blu. Thank you again."

"I just wish you would tell Chief Pitman the truth."

"I am. I am." He sighed heavily. "It's something you probably won't ever understand, but I am."

Blu wanted to question him further but she could see the exhaustion in the droop of his eyelids. "Alright, Gill. We'll talk more tomorrow. Okay?"

"Sure."

CHAPTER 18

As Blu left the room her heart was tugged in several directions. A part of her wanted to be able to walk him right out of the police station with her. Unfortunately, a small part of her had begun to wonder if Gill might be guilty after all.

"So? What do you think?" Chief Pitman stood near the door.

Blu looked past him and saw the kids playing with tin badges.

"I'm not sure. He didn't tell me anything more than what he told you."

"Well, great. It's not like I want to keep an innocent man in jail, but if he doesn't even claim his innocence, then I don't know what to do. We're going to have to keep him at least until the end of the hold, then charge him."

"I'll see what I can come up with." Blu frowned. She knew that there wasn't much chance that she'd find anything solid, but she could hope. "He did ask for me to get him a few things from his house."

"I have a key. The house is part of the investigation, but it's already been processed. I can lead the way over if you want."

"Yes that would be great. Hey, thanks for giving the kids a tour."

"Sure, no problem. I think they enjoyed it."

"Put your hands up, Blu! You're going down!" Joey pointed his fingers in the shape of a gun at Blu.

"No. No, don't do that, Joey!" Blu laughed. "I think they learned a lot."

"Oops—is that not allowed any more?" Chief Pitman grinned. "When AJ was a boy I used to play cops and robbers with him all the time. Of course, I always had to be the robber."

Blu smiled at him. Prior to that day she would never have been able to picture Chief Pitman chasing around a young AJ for the fun of it. Now she understood the Uncle Paul that AJ saw. He wasn't as gruff and cold as he pretended to be at times.

"I'm sure it will be fine. If he gets kicked out of school, I'll blame it on you." She laughed.

Blu led the kids out to the parking lot. "Well, you've had quite an adventurous morning. Was it fun playing with Chief Pitman?"

"He locked me up!" Marley hopped into her car seat. "Like a bad guy!"

"Oh boy." Blu cringed. "I wonder what your Mommy is going to say when she hears about that."

Once the kids were buckled in Blu got into the driver's seat. She was about to start the engine when her cell phone rang. She glanced around the parking lot but did not see Chief Pitman's car just yet.

When she saw that it was Maddie calling, she answered the phone. "Hi, Maddie. What's up?"

"While you were with the chief I did some searching for you. When I searched the Peddles' name, I found nothing—which isn't entirely surprising, as most people over a certain age don't leave much of a digital footprint. However, when I searched the name of the ice cream shop—Peddle's Ice Cream Shop—I found something strange."

"What?"

"There are five ice cream shops by the same name. One other in this state and three more in surrounding states."

"That is rather odd. Were you able to tell who owned them?"

"That's where it gets even more interesting. I was able to trace the owners of all four of the other ice cream shops back to the Peddles. One is owned by a nephew, another by a distant cousin, and the third is owned by a great-niece."

"What about the fourth?"

"The fourth is an odd one. The name is Jarod Peddle, but I can't figure out how he's related to Gill and Martha."

"Interesting. Well, they are relatives, so they may want to know of Martha's passing."

"Can I come over and tell you what I found out in more detail?"

"Sure, that would be great. I'm stopping by Gill's house to see if I can pick up a few of the things he needs, then I'll be home. I'll text you when we get there."

"Okay. Sounds good.

Blu hung up the phone and followed Chief Pitman out of the parking lot.

As she drove she noticed that there was a man walking down the street in the opposite direction. At first she thought he was the real estate agent, because he had a camera hanging around his neck. Then she noticed that he looked quite a bit older than the other man. She shook her head and focused on driving.

Chief Pitman stopped at a quaint cottage that was about three streets away from the beach. Blu could see Martha's touch all over it, as a garden rambled from the corners of the house right up to the street. There were tiny little statues mixed in with the bushy flowers.

Chief Pitman walked up to the side of her car. "I'll unlock the door, then stay with the kids while you go inside."

"Thanks a lot."

He walked up the short path and unlocked the front door, then walked back to the car. "Just don't take too long. I do have somewhere else I need to be soon."

"Okay, I won't."

CHAPTER 19

Blu pushed the door to the house open. It felt strange to walk into someone's house without being invited. Even though she felt so close to the Peddles, she'd never actually been inside their home before.

Just like outside, Martha's taste sprawled throughout the house from afghans on the couch to doilies on the side tables. She noticed that Gill had one little corner that was dedicated to sports memorabilia, not for one particular team, but for all of the games he had attended. Blu smiled as she looked it over, but she knew that she couldn't linger long.

A large picture of the couple—perhaps when they'd been in their sixties or so—hung over the fireplace. Their hands were intertwined and their shoulders touched—not in a pose, but in what looked like a very natural stance for them. That was not the type of couple that ended with one of them murdering the other. Blu couldn't help the thought that solidified everything she thought she already knew about the couple.

Blu found a few books that looked like they might

belong to Gill. Then she started to look for his shoes. They weren't by the front door. She walked to the master bedroom. The bed was made. The curtains were drawn.

Blu's heart flipped as she realized that the bed had not been slept in since Martha's death. For a brief moment Blu thought she could sense Martha there with her.

"Who did this to you, Martha? Who took you from him?"

She opened the closet door with the intention of looking for the shoes, but also to snoop. On the floor of the closet were several shoeboxes. Blu opened one to find that it was filled with paperwork, not shoes.

She noticed that each of the boxes had a label on it—Peddle 1, Peddle 2, and Peddle 3. She frowned. It was an odd way to keep records, but nothing that was going to point her toward a killer.

She pushed the boxes aside and looked behind them. She noticed that in one corner of the closet the carpet lifted up. Curious, she pulled it back. There was a large photograph in a plastic ziplock bag. Blu pulled it out to take a closer look.

The face itself was so shadowed that she couldn't make much out, but the figure appeared to be in his teens. She wasn't sure what to think about it. Why would the Peddles go to so much trouble to hide this particular photograph?

A knock at the door reminded her that Chief Pitman

was still waiting for her. She turned away and started to leave the bedroom when she bumped into a large sewing table. A pile of yarn toppled over. As she began to gather the yarn she noticed something that appeared to be hidden beneath the yarn. She was curious about what was underneath.

When she got to the bottom of the pile there was a large embroidery that looked like a photograph. Only half of the face was etched into the material, with a needle pinned where Martha had left off. A wave of sadness caused Blu's eyes to prick with tears.

"I'm sorry that you never had a chance to finish this, Martha."

She piled the yarn back up and looked around the room for any sign of Gill's shoes.

"Blu, let's go. I have to get home."

"Okay, I'm just looking for the shoes."

"Maybe by the back door?"

Blu nodded and walked through the house to the back door. When she reached it, she saw no shoes by the door. She was crushed. The one thing Gill had asked her for she wasn't going to be able to provide.

When she stepped back out of the house she shook her head. "They aren't there, or at least I can't find them."

"Well, maybe he can tell you where they are exactly the next time you see him. Until then we really need to get going. I'm supposed to be meeting Shawna this afternoon to help her move her artwork from the basement for the art show tomorrow."

"Shawna? She lives with you?"

"Yes."

"Oh. Is there a reason?" Blu knew that she was being nosy, but she couldn't help herself asking now that the chief seemed to be warming up to her a bit more.

"It's not my story to tell, Blu. Remember, keep me up-to-date on anything that you find." He locked the door, then tipped his hat at her.

"Yes, I will."

Blu got into the driver's seat of the car and started the engine. Joey and Marley were restless in the backseat.

"Marley, stop poking me or I'll arrest you!"

Blu drove back to the beach house, anxious to get the kids home where they could play.

Blu texted Maddie to let her know that they were home, then prepared a quick lunch for the children.

Her mind circled the events of the day piece by piece. As she set a cup of orange juice in front of Joey, she thought about the amount of times Martha and Gill must have shared a meal.

She was certain that he wouldn't have gone to all the trouble of luring her outside behind the dumpster. So who did? Was it the woman from the mall? Was it the real estate agent, in the hopes of rattling her? It seemed a little extreme to Blu to think of a real estate agent killing someone who stood in his way, but then he had said that he didn't get to where he was by being nice.

Blu turned toward a knock on the front door. "You two stay put. I'll be right back."

CHAPTER 20

Blu left the kitchen to open the front door.

Maddie walked in with her laptop in hand.

"Where are the kids?" Blu looked past her.

"It's family fun day so Penelope has them for the day. Wait until you see what I found."

"What is it?"

Maddie set her laptop on the kitchen table for both Blu and her to look at.

"Using the addresses of each of the shops, I managed to find pictures of them. I tried finding them on maps first, but there weren't any pictures. Then I stumbled across this treasure trove." She clicked on a link and a website opened up.

"Whoever runs this site has an interest in photography. He has thousands of pictures on here, as well as one of each of our ice cream shops."

"Including Gill's?"

Maddie clicked on another link.

Blu stared at the picture. She recognized the image right away from the one of hers that she and Maddie had been looking at the other day.

"I think it's the picture that he took when yours was taken. I think he just cropped out everything but the name of the shop and the roof," said Maddie.

"I wonder why?"

"See that." Maddie pointed to a tiny ribbon of light.

"That's right where the horseshoe would have been!"

"Exactly. Now look at these." Maddie pulled up the pictures of the other shops. On each of the pictures just below the sign for the shop, there were horseshoes.

"Look at this—there are horseshoes on the front of each of these buildings. They're not hidden like the one on the Peddles' shop was."

"Horseshoes? What kind of sense does that make?" Maddie shook her head. "It's an odd decoration for an ice cream shop."

"Not if it's an ice cream shop for horses." Marley giggled.

"Can horses eat ice cream?" Maddie tapped a finger against her chin. "I've never really thought about that."

Marley laughed harder.

"Marley, horseshoes are also seen as a symbol of good luck. That's why Mr. Peddle has one on his shop." Blu smiled at her.

"So he put them on all of the shops?"

"Well, if he's connected to these shops, somehow then I guess he did. I think he also has one tattooed on his arm, but I couldn't see the whole thing."

"Huh. Pretty superstitious, I guess."

"If these people are related to the Peddles, why haven't any of them come to town after Martha's death?"

"Not everyone is close to their family." Maddie shrugged. "Maybe they're distant enough relatives that they don't feel the need to make that type of connection."

"Maybe. It's an odd connection for them to all have an ice cream shop with the same name but not be close enough to even be concerned about Martha—or Gill, for that matter."

"There's only one way to find out for sure. I can get you the contact information for all of the current owners. Then you can go from there."

"What about the name of the photographer? It must be the same man that was in my photograph. Is there any way to find out who he is?"

"As far as I can tell, it's not one of the owners of the ice cream shops. It must just be an admirer. I'm afraid my tech savvy has its limits. I'm sure there's a way, but I don't know how. There isn't even an e-mail address to contact him on the website—no name, no identifying information at all. His photographs are from all over the country, so that doesn't even give me a clue as to where he might live."

"Hm. Maybe the police could find more information?"

"Maybe. Give Chief Pitman a call and give him the website."

"I'm sure he'll think it's a long shot, but he did say to share information."

"I'll let you make that call. I have to pick up a few things and I have an appointment at the salon. Just call me if you need anything. I should be able to have that contact information to you soon."

"Thanks, Maddie. Just send it when you get it. Then I'll start making calls. Someone has to know something about all of this."

"You know the one person who knows everything about it."

"Yes, I do. Gill, but he's not talking." Blu sighed.

She began to gather the lunch dishes. Maddie left and the kids settled on the floor in the living room with a deck of cards.

Blu dialed Chief Pitman's phone number.

"Hello? I'm in the middle of something."

"I'm sorry to interrupt, Chief Pitman. I had some information that you might want to know about."

"That's great, because I have some information too."

"You go first."

"You're not going to like it."

Blu frowned. "What is it?"

"I had the tests run on that shoe. It is blueberry on the shoe."

"Okay. Well, we expected that."

"Yes, we did, but what we didn't expect was that the shoe would belong to Gill."

"What? His missing shoes? Someone must have stolen them."

Chief Pitman sighed heavily. "Blu, that's what you may think but a jury is going to think that Gill tried to ditch his shoes after killing his wife."

"You know that's not true. Clearly someone is framing him. This must be very personal."

"I'm trying here, Blu, but every shred of evidence is pointing directly at Gill."

"I have a website to show you. I'm going to text you the link. On it are photographs of ice cream shops, all with the same name as Gill's. They're in different states."

"What does that matter?"

"Well, the owners all have some kind of connection to Gill, even if it's distant, except for one. There are also horseshoes on each of the buildings."

"Horseshoes? What does that matter?"

Blu remembered that she hadn't yet told Chief Pitman about the horseshoes, or about the photograph with a man taking a picture of the ice cream shop. "There's a horseshoe on the roof of the Peddles' shop. It's hidden."

"I knew it! I knew AJ was hiding something from me the other day. You were up on that roof the whole time, weren't you?"

"I was. But don't be upset with AJ. I asked him not to tell anyone. I didn't think the horseshoe meant anything at the time."

"Well, it sounds like it might now."

"I believe that Gill also has a horseshoe tattooed on his arm."

"He does. Get this, it has his own name on it."

"He had his own name tattooed onto his body?"

"Yes. We documented it when he was brought in."

"Do you think your techs can find out who this website belongs to?"

"I can try. But I don't see why we need to know that."

"Just trust me on this one."

"I will, Blu, but pretty soon I'm going to have to officially press charges against Gill. I can't hold off much longer."

"I'll see what I can find out."

CHAPTER 21

Blu spent the afternoon doing some research of her own. When Maddie sent her the e-mail with contact information for each of the owners of the shops, she didn't hesitate to get to work. The kids were occupied with a movie, and Blu was ready to make some progress on the case. She set up shop on the dining room table so she could keep an eye on the kids and also make her calls.

Blu called the first name on the list—Vance Peddle.

"Hello?"

"Hello, Vance? My name is Blu and—"

"—I don't want to buy anything."

"I'm not selling anything. I'm calling you about your cousin— Gill Peddle?"

"Who?"

"Gill Peddle. He owns an ice cream shop too."

"Oh. I'm sorry I don't know him."

"Are you sure? Your ice cream shops have the exact same name."

"Well, Peddle is probably a pretty common name.

Anyway, I didn't name the shop."

"Would you mind telling me who did?"

"We got this letter in the mail with all of the deed information and the money needed to open the shop. Actually, it was sent to my mother, but she put it in my name. I've been running it ever since."

"Do you think I could speak to your mother about it?"

"I'm afraid you can't. She passed away three years ago."

"I'm sorry for your loss."

"Thank you. This shop is all I have left of her, so I'm not even going to think about selling it."

"Oh, I'm not calling for that reason."

"Good. I've had some strange character skulking around here trying to take pictures and make offers. I told him I had no interest."

"Really? Do you know the name of the real estate agent?"

"I threw him off of my property. His name was Ken."

Blu's eyes widened. Was it possible that the same real estate agent was trying to buy another Peddle ice cream shop in an entirely different state?

"And you're sure you've never heard of Gill or Martha Peddle?"

"I'm afraid not. I don't have much family."

"Alright, thank you for your time." Blu hung up the phone before Vance could question her further.

Her mind raced as she wondered what Ken might be up to. She recalled that he'd said that he was looking out for the interests of his client. Who was his client?

She placed a quick call to Maddie.

"Did you find anything?" Maddie asked as soon as she picked up the phone.

"I'm not sure yet. I was wondering if you could work your magic on a real estate agent named Ken Buchman. Can you find out what his specialty is and who he might have as a client?"

"I'll see what I can do and e-mail you what I find."

"Thanks, Maddie!"

Blu hung up the phone and continued to make calls to the current owners of the ice cream shops. As she went down through her list she heard many similar stories. All of the shops had been left to the people now running them by a distant or estranged relative— someone they claimed not to know at all. None had ever met Gill or Martha, or even been to their ice cream shop. When she got to the last name on the list, Jarod Peddle, she wondered what his story would be.

He picked up on the second ring.

"Hello?"

"Hi, is this Jarod Peddle?"

"Yes, it is."

"My name is Blu, and I'm calling about your ice cream shop."

"Oh, it's closed today."

"That's fine. I was actually calling to speak with you. I was wondering if you are familiar with a man named Gill Peddle."

"No. Well, not really. I mean he left me the ice cream shop."

Blu's eyes widened. Jarod was the first person she found who had a direct connection with Gill.

"So you do know him?"

"I've never met him. I just found out that he left me the shop."

"Gill Peddle did?"

"Yes he did."

"But Gill Peddle is still alive." Blu shook her head.

"Oh. Does he want the shop back?"

Jarod sounded anxious.

Blu blinked and tightened her grip on the phone. "How old are you, Jarod?"

"Twenty."

"That's a little young to be running your own shop."

"I know. I mean, when my dad left it to me, I thought it was weird. I never even met the guy."

"Your dad? Gill Peddle is your dad?"

"Sure. I guess. That's what the birth certificate says."

Blu's heart pounded. In her wildest notions she never expected to discover that Gill might have cheated on Martha. None of what Jarod was saying made sense to her. Her mind spun with the revelation. Then she began to think it through. The Gill Peddle she knew was well into his eighties, and though it was possible that he had fathered a son twenty years prior, she didn't think it was very likely. Was it possible that he was talking about a different Gill Peddle, or someone using his name?

"Do you know how old your father was?"

"He was forty-two when he died, a long time ago, but I guess his will just got settled. At least I thought it did. I told my mom it might be some kind of scam, but she said that it was real. So now the shop is mine—unless, I mean, it's not."

"I'm sorry, Jarod. The Gill Peddle I was speaking of is in his eighties. I don't think he's the same man."

"Oh." Jarod sighed. "Well, I guess that's for the best. I mean, either way, it doesn't make much of a difference to me, but I kind of like running the ice cream shop. It makes people happy. I like that."

"Jarod, has anyone tried to buy the shop from you?"

"Yes, about two weeks ago. This real slimy guy showed up and offered my mom and me cash to buy the shop. He said he had a client that was very interested and that price was no object."

"Wow. But you declined?"

"My mom questioned him about it, and I guess he told her something that she didn't like, so she threw him out of the shop and told him not to come back. She was pretty upset after that."

"Do you think I could talk to your mom?"

"Oh, she's not here now. She had to go on a trip.

She's been gone about three days. But I can give her a message when she gets back if you want."

"No, that's okay." Blu's heart skipped a beat. "Thanks for your time, Jarod."

"Sure. I mean, if that guy wants his ice cream shop back, just let me know."

"I'm sure it will be fine. Thanks, Jarod."

CHAPTER 22

Blu hung up the phone and stared down at the paper she had been taking notes on. It was pretty obvious to her that Jarod's mother had something to do with this. She was on vacation? Could she have been the woman who confronted Martha in the mall?

"Blu, look what I made!" Marley held up a picture that she'd drawn.

"Oh, Marley, that's beautiful." Blu tried to decipher the swirls and shapes. "Is it a building?"

"Yes! It's an ice cream shop!"

"Very nice, Marley. We should take that to the art show tomorrow, okay?"

"Yay!" Marley grinned. "Maybe I will win a prize."

"I'll take you for ice—" She paused just before making a promise that she couldn't keep. She wouldn't be able to take Marley for ice cream. The ice cream shop would be closed. Gill would still be in jail. Blu would not wake up to a solved crime. "Don't worry, we'll make sure that we get a treat. Okay?"

"Okay." Marley smiled. "I'm going to add a horse!"

"Good idea."

Blu sat back in her chair and looked at the notes she'd made. The information she had only left her more confused. But she was quite curious about Jarod's mother. At Jarod's age and with his location she could easily find him on social media.

She began the hunt and as she expected, Jarod was not difficult to find. Although many of his profiles were blocked, she was able to connect enough dots to figure out the name of his mother.

"Erica Grimes." She frowned. The fact that Jarod's mother and he did not share the same last name meant that perhaps she'd never been married to Jarod's father. Maybe she just told Jarod a story about who his father was. After all, he had said that he'd never met the man.

Blu tapped her pencil against the paper. So if Jarod was really Gill's son, that meant that Erica was his ex-lover. If Erica was the woman who Blu saw arguing with Martha at the mall, then there was a good chance that they were arguing about Gill's and Erica's past. It made Blu sick to her stomach to think that a man like Gill could make such a mistake, but then it wasn't that uncommon for a spouse to stray.

She did a little more searching for Erica's name and managed to find a picture of her. As she suspected, she looked like the woman who had been at the mall with Martha. Blu had been some distance away when she'd seen her, though, so it was still possible that it wasn't the same person.

There was only one way to know for sure.

If Jarod claimed that Erica was on vacation, then she would have needed a place to stay. Since she wasn't here for fun, and might not have a lot of money to spend, Blu guessed that she would pick a lower-priced hotel or motel.

She did a search for the hotels and motels that were closest to the Peddles' house. Since they lived close to the beach, there were quite a few to choose from. Blu stretched her arms, checked on the kids, and then settled in to make the calls.

She called the first motel and asked for Erica by name. Eight hotels later she began to feel discouraged. Maybe her entire theory was wrong. She decided to call at least one more before she had to make dinner.

"Beachside Rooms."

"Is this a hotel?"

"It's a boarding house."

"Oh." Blu frowned. She wasn't sure if Erica would stay in a place as small as that but it didn't hurt to ask. "Could I speak with Erica Grimes?"

"One second." After a pause the voice came back on the line. "She's not in right now. Would you like me to leave her a message?"

Blu's heart raced. "Uh, no, that's okay. Actually I was supposed to meet her but I forgot what room she is staying in."

"Room eight."

"Thanks."

"Would you like me to let her know that you called?"

"No, that's okay. Thank you for your help." Blu hung up the phone.

She couldn't believe that the pieces seemed to be fitting together. Erica, Jarod's mother, was in town, and she had been in town for at least three days, which meant she could have easily poisoned Martha.

She picked up the phone to call Maddie to give her an update and then noticed two hungry faces staring at her.

"Blu? When is dinner? It's dark outside."

Blu grimaced as she realized that she'd been so caught up in her search that quite a bit of time had passed.

"I'm making it right now."

Blu prepared their dinner as her mind flipped through what she knew.

By the time the kids had eaten, bathed, and got tucked into bed, Blu thought it was too late to call Maddie or Chief Pitman.

She decided that first thing in the morning she would let them both know what she'd found out. Blu could only hope that it would be enough to take some of the suspicion off Gill.

CHAPTER 23

When Blu woke up the next morning, the first thing she did was reach for her phone. She called Chief Pitman first. When she filled him in on what she'd found out about Erica, he seemed to be listening intently.

"That's very good information. If it checks out, we might be able to use it."

"Do you think it will be enough to delay charges against Gill?"

"I honestly don't know for sure. It may be, but it's going to take some fancy paperwork on my part."

"Just do your best to keep him from being officially charged, Chief. You know what that will do to his reputation."

"I do know. We're on the same side, Blu. Just remember that."

Blu hung up the phone and called Maddie to update her.

"I think that Erica is the killer. She must have come here to confront Gill about his son and ended up confronting Martha instead."

"But why would she kill Martha?"

"I don't know. Maybe she was jealous of her and wanted to be with Gill?"

"Maybe." Maddie's voice trailed off. "I don't know, though. It just seems odd to me. Could Gill have kept that secret for twenty years?"

"Maybe. Or maybe Martha knew about it. Maybe that's why they never expanded. Gill might have been using the money to support his son or to silence relatives that knew about him."

"No, it just doesn't add up to me."

"I'll find out more when I speak to Erica. I have to take the kids to the art show first. Are you going?"

"No, Brennan thinks it's lame and Chrissa is meeting up with her friends. Let me know if there's anything I can do to help."

"I will. Bye, Maddie."

She hung up the phone and went into Marley's room to wake her up.

As she helped her get dressed Marley yawned.

"Is the art show today?"

"Yes. I'm looking forward to it. Aren't you?"

"I would be if we could get ice cream!"

"Don't worry. How about if we stop for cupcakes?"

"Oh yes! Okay!" Marley bounded off into the kitchen for breakfast.

Blu smiled a little at how fast her mood could change.

As she prepared their breakfast she had a hard time staying focused. Her mind shifted back to Gill and Martha. Could she really have been so wrong about their love? Was it all just a front? She didn't even want to think about the possibility.

As she gathered the kids to head out to the art show, her phone rang. She was in the middle of buckling Marley in her car seat, so she ignored it. Then she started to drive before she'd remembered that her phone had rung. She drove to the art show and parked.

When she checked her phone she saw that the call was from Chief Pitman. She hit redial but was greeted by his voicemail message. She double-checked her own voicemail to see that he hadn't left one for her.

"Here we are. Let's check out some wonderful art, kids."

She led the children into the local recreational center that hosted the art show. Marley bolted straight for the brightly decorated kids' section where she could put her picture on display. As Blu and Joey caught up with her, a familiar voice greeted them.

"Morning. It's good to see you." AJ held out a few brochures to them.

"I didn't know you were part of this." Blu smiled and took a brochure. "Thanks."

"Well, since I've never been much of an artist myself I like to be around it. You know, so maybe some will rub off on me."

"Only if the paint is still wet!" Marley giggled.

"Good point, Marley." AJ patted the top of her head. "There's a lot of interesting pieces to see. There's even a photography section that you might want to look at."

"Okay, we'll do that. Do you want to join us?"

"Sorry, I can't. I have to man the front. But maybe later we could have a rematch on the beach?" He looked at the two children. "I've got a big shovel this time."

"I have a big shovel!" Marley jumped up and down.

"My shovel is bigger!" AJ grinned.

"Please, Blu, can we?" Joey looked up at her.

"Actually that would be perfect. I hate to ask again, AJ, but maybe I could leave them with you for a few minutes?"

"Of course. But, uh, I'm going to start expecting payment."

"Oh sure, of course. Twenty?" She reached into her purse.

"Blu, I'm not going to take money from you. But I wouldn't mind sharing a meal."

Blu nodded. She was in no position to argue. "Okay, dinner it is."

"Really?" He raised an eyebrow. "Should I have you sign something?"

"Ha-ha." Blu grinned. "Let's go, kids."

AJ winked at her as she walked away. Blu couldn't ignore the flutter of her stomach at the thought of spending some time alone with AJ.

As they walked through the exhibits she had a hard time paying attention to the artwork. Her mind kept returning to Erica. Had Chief Pitman followed up on the lead? Had he ignored it? She pulled out her phone and tried to call him again. Once more it went to his voicemail.

CHAPTER 24

When they entered the photography section of the art show, Blu's attention was captured by a photograph on the wall.

"Look at this, Marley. It's a clown." Joey tugged his sister a few steps away to another photograph, but Blu couldn't look away from the one in front of her.

"Do you like it?"

Blu turned to look at the man beside her. He wore a low baseball cap, a baggy windbreaker, and a pair of whitewashed jeans that told his age more than his youthful features did.

"There's something about it. It feels familiar somehow."

He nodded as he studied the picture as well. "It could be Anytown USA, right?"

"Look at this." She pointed to the corner of a sign that could barely be seen in the photograph. "Can you make out the letters?"

"Oh." He cleared his throat. "It's an ice cream shop."

Blu's eyes widened. "Are you sure?"

"Yes."

"How can you be so sure?" Blu tilted her head from side to side as she tried to get the right angle.

"Because I'm the one that took the picture." He chuckled.

Blu looked back at him as she took a sharp breath.

"You are?"

"I'm sorry, I didn't mean to troll for compliments. It's just that so few people have ever gazed at my work like that before. I was curious to know what it was that held the attention of a young woman like yourself."

Blu narrowed her eyes. "What's the name of the ice cream shop?"

"Peddle's."

"Like the one here in town?"

"Ah, yes. But this is a different one. In another state."

Blu inched a few steps away from him. "Why did you take a picture of it?"

"I find the story behind it intriguing. I take pictures of interesting things—not just beautiful, but novel. You know?"

"What's so interesting about the ice cream shop?"

"Oh, I thought you saw it."

"Saw what?"

He pointed to the peak of the roof. "See that?"

Blu squinted her eyes. She could just make out the horseshoe. "Oh wow! I didn't see that at first."

"Yes, that's the interesting part. There are five

Peddle's Ice Cream Shops and each one has a horseshoe."

"How did you discover that?"

"I used to vacation here. I was here when Mr. Peddle opened his ice cream shop for the first time. I watched him nail that horseshoe to his roof, where no one could see it. When I asked him why he did it, he put his finger to his lips and told me that it was a secret." The man put his fingers to his lips to show Blu. "It made my curiosity and my imagination go wild. My family traveled a lot over the years, and I noticed there was another Peddle's Ice Cream Shop. When I researched the shops, I found that there were five in total. I wanted to know if the ice cream shops were all connected, so a year ago I went on a photography journey and snapped pictures of all the other shops. Apparently my idea was very popular. I've been paid quite a bit of money for my pictures."

"Were you here last year? Did you take a picture then?" Blu searched his eyes.

"Yes. I did." He sighed. "That was before." His lips drooped and his eyes narrowed.

"Before what?"

"Well, you know. Gill killed Martha."

The words struck Blu hard. She wasn't sure what she expected to hear from the man, but it was not that.

"I don't believe he did it."

"Who would? He was a sweet old guy. I'm sure the police will figure it out." He shrugged.

"Did you know them?"

"No. Not at all. I liked to think I got to know them a little through my photographs. But can anyone ever really know someone?" He tilted his head to the side. "I'd never imagine that there was a monster living in an ice cream shop."

Blu frowned. "You can't always believe what you hear."

"That's the truth." He chuckled. "I'm Harry, by the way." He offered her his hand.

Blu shook it.

He held her hand for a moment longer than necessary, then released it. "I'd love to hear your opinions on the rest of my work, by the way—good or bad."

Blu steered the kids along with her as she studied each photograph. She found that Harry was very easy to talk to.

"How come there are so many shadows in your pictures?" She looked over at him. "Do you find the world to be hidden, or are you hiding from it?"

"A little of both." He smiled. "I find it difficult to find my place in the world. I would guess that it's somewhere between the shadows and the light."

"How poetic."

"You think?" He laughed. "Sometimes it still shocks me that people even like my work. To me, they're just pictures of the world I see."

"It's a beautiful world."

"Blu, are we going to the beach?" Joey leaned against

the wall. "I'm bored."

"Sorry." Blu cringed. "They're not exactly art experts."

"It's fine." Harry looked at the two kids. "I wouldn't want to keep you from the real beauty in life. Nature—that's the art you should enjoy." He smiled at Blu. "Would you mind if I tagged along?"

"Not at all. That would be nice." Blu smiled back as he fell into step beside her.

She was tempted to tell him about the pictures she found on his website, but she didn't want him to know that she had been searching for him. As they left the recreational center Blu looked for AJ. She didn't see him, but assumed that he might already be down at the beach.

When they reached the water, Blu looked around for AJ again. Again, she saw no sign of him.

"Do you live around here, Harry?"

"I don't. I live far away from all this. I came because I was invited to display my art. I guess a part of me wanted to see the ice cream shop that started it all again. Now I wish I hadn't."

"Because of the tragedy?"

"Yes—because of the tragedy. I used to think that life couldn't get better than a little ice cream shop, but now I see life inside the ice cream shop wasn't that great either."

"I think someone framed Gill. I don't think he killed Martha."

"Hm." He shrugged. "That's quite a story."

Blu looked out over the water. "Yes, it is."

She smiled as Marley splashed a bit of water in her direction.

"Could I take your picture?"

Blu turned to face him and quirked an eyebrow. "Why?"

"Because you look just perfect in that light. The way you smile when you're looking at the children. It's really beautiful, and I'd love to be able to capture it."

Blu laughed a little. "Well, I guess it couldn't hurt."

"Good. But don't pose. Just go back to what you were doing. It's not the same unless you're not expecting it."

CHAPTER 25

Blu looked back at the children racing up and down along the sand. It wasn't long before she was so wrapped up in their activity that she didn't even notice Harry's camera clicking away. It wasn't until she heard heavy footsteps running up to her that she was rattled out of her peaceful state.

"What do you think you're doing?" AJ scowled at Harry as he stepped between Blu and the camera.

Harry backed up so fast that he tripped over his own feet and landed hard in the sand. "I'm sorry, I'm sorry. Don't hurt me."

"AJ!" Blu grabbed him hard by the arm. "I told him it was okay. Why are you acting like this?"

AJ looked from Blu to the man in the sand. Then he looked back at Blu again. "I'm sorry. It looked like he was sneaking around. I didn't know that you knew what he was doing."

"Maybe ask a question first next time?" Blu frowned. She reached out her hand to Harry, who got to his feet. He watched AJ warily as he brushed the sand from his pants.

"I didn't mean any harm. Is this your boyfriend?"

"No." Blu narrowed eyes. "We're just friends."

AJ's lips drew into a thin stern line. He shook his head. "I'm really sorry. I misread the situation. I hope you aren't hurt."

"I'm fine, it's okay." Harry lowered his eyes.

Blu wrapped her arm around his. He was so soft-spoken and meek compared to AJ that she felt the need to shield him from the larger man's wrath.

"Blu, I'm sorry." AJ met her eyes, though his jaw rippled with tension at the sight of her arm wrapped around Harry's. "I didn't mean to cause any trouble. I shouldn't have jumped to conclusions."

"You're sure you're not hurt? Your camera?" Blu frowned.

"I promise, I'm okay. Mistakes happen." He offered AJ a cordial smile.

"AJ, maybe you keeping an eye on the kids isn't such a good idea."

"It's fine, Blu. I'm sorry. I just got overprotective."

"Are you sure? I know I might be asking too much."

"Does payment still stand?" AJ winked.

Blu smiled. "Yes."

"Then I'm sure. I don't want to miss my chance to bury these little scoundrels."

"Thanks, AJ." Blu turned back to Harry. "Harry, I

have to get going."

"I'll walk you back up to your car." Harry smiled.

Blu wondered how he knew that she'd driven there, but she didn't question him. She walked back to the parking lot with Harry at her side. She glanced back once to see AJ playing with the kids.

A twinge of guilt caused her to flinch. AJ was only trying to protect her, but she didn't appreciate how aggressive he was. Harry couldn't be more harmless, and she hated to think that he might have been hurt by AJ causing a scene.

"Are you sure that you're okay, Harry?"

"I'm fine, really. I just hope that the pictures aren't ruined." He smiled at her. "I guess I'm not the only one who can see how perfect you are."

Blu's cheeks burned at his words. She didn't think that there was much perfect about her, but she did wonder what might have gotten under AJ's skin.

"It was nice meeting you, Harry."

"I hope that we'll get the chance to see each other again."

"Are you in town for long?"

"I've been here a week. I leave tomorrow."

"Oh, so you've been here for some time?" Blu studied him.

"Yes, I wanted to spend some time on the beach."

"I hope to see you again before you leave. I have an appointment I have to get to now."

"I don't want to hold you up." He held her gaze. "I will see you again."

"Okay." Blu smiled again and climbed into her car.

She didn't have much time to get to the boarding house, as she didn't want to leave the kids with AJ for too long.

Blu tried yet again to call Chief Pitman. She wanted to know whether he had gone ahead and charged Gill or if he'd released him. When she heard his voicemail again she hung up with a jab of her finger. Either he was avoiding her or he forgot to charge his phone. She thought about swinging by the station, but her mind was too focused on Erica.

If she'd already checked out, then there was a good chance Blu would never be able to find her, and she had no idea if Chief Pitman had followed up on the information she'd given him. She stepped into the lobby of what was actually a large house, rather than a motel. A skinny sleepy man sat behind the front desk.

"Room eight?"

He lifted a hand and pointed down a hallway without speaking a word.

Blu made her way down the hallway to the room with an eight on the door. She was about to knock when she noticed that the door was slightly open.

"I'm coming home today, Jarod. I can't believe that you told some random person on the phone so much about us. Are you sure she asked about Gill?" There was a pause and then Erica continued. "Don't worry about it, Jarod. It's just a little complicated. Things didn't exactly go as I'd planned. I'll be home soon. Don't answer the phone or the door for anyone. I'm serious."

Blu lifted an eyebrow. To her, it sounded as if Erica was afraid of someone. Did she expect that the police would be looking for her?

CHAPTER 26

Blu lifted her hand again to knock on the door, but before she could, Erica jerked it open and nearly walked into her.

"Excuse me." She narrowed her eyes. "Who are you?"

"My name is Blu."

"Are you the one that called my son?"

"I did." Blu searched her eyes. "Are you the one who killed Martha Peddle?"

"How dare you!" Erica shoved past her. "I had nothing to do with that. I never should have come here. It was a mistake."

"Well, you can't leave."

"I can and I am."

"Wait! Erica, what are you going to tell your son? That you're a murderer?"

"I didn't murder anyone." She spun around to face Blu. "I didn't. Gill's the one who killed someone, not me."

"Gill wouldn't do that to Martha."

"Ha—then you don't know Gill very well. He's a terrible man and they lied to me about him."

"They who?" Blu blinked.

"Martha and Gill."

"Wait, are you saying Gill lied to you about Gill?

"Oh, you're wasting my time! I have to get home to Jarod to make sure that he's safe."

Erica was already out the door when Blu caught up with her. Blu reached for her arm to stop her, but Erica raised her hands into the air.

"Don't move!"

Blu looked up to see Chief Pitman with his gun pointed at Erica. Blu lifted her hands into the air as well.

"Chief Pitman, what's going on?"

"Erica Grimes, you're under arrest for the murder of Martha Peddle."

"What? No! You can't do this! I didn't do anything! It was him! It was Gill!"

"Let's go." Chief Pitman handed her off to a waiting officer. Once Erica was led away, he turned to look at Blu.

"That information you gave us checked out. We also had an eyewitness who said that Martha and Erica were seen walking together on the beach the morning of the murder. I had to decide whether to charge or release Gill, so I released him. I hope your instincts are right on this one, Blu."

"I know they are." Blu stared after Erica with

confidence.

"It's a strange turn of events. I guess Gill confessed in some attempt to protect his ex-lover."

"So Jarod is his?"

"It's not confirmed yet, but he does share his last name. I'm sure Erica will be willing to tell us the whole story. It's over, Blu. At least now you can rest well knowing that you protected Gill from being put away for murder."

"Yes." Blu nodded. "I can't wait to go speak with him."

"I released him this morning. He should be home."

"I tried calling you to let you know I was coming here."

"I know—my phone was buzzing all day. I couldn't find a minute to get back to you. I had to do a lot of paperwork and call in some favors to get Gill released and Erica in handcuffs."

"You did a good job, Chief Pitman."

"With your help, Nanny Blu."

"It's just Blu."

"Sure." He nodded.

As he walked away, Blu expected to feel calm. Instead, her heart pounded harder than ever. She was sure that once she saw Gill everything would be fine.

When she returned to the beach AJ was buried in the sand yet again.

"I thought things were supposed to happen the other way around this time?" Blu laughed.

"What can I say? They have a way with words."

"I bet." Blu grinned. "Let's go, you two. I did promise you cupcakes, remember?"

"Cupcakes!" The kids jumped up out of the sand.

AJ managed to break free of the sand as well.

"Do you want to come with us?" Blu automatically reached up and helped him brush some sand from his skin. She froze when she realized what she'd done.

AJ caught her hand. "I'm not going to let you pass off a cupcake as dinner."

"Would I do that?" Blu grinned.

"Absolutely." He gave her hand a little squeeze and then released it.

"You should know that your uncle released Gill. He has another suspect in custody."

"That's great. I'm sure it was because of your detective work."

"I like to think I might have helped." She grinned, but the expression faded. "Although she doesn't seem the type to be a murderer."

"A murderer doesn't wear some kind of sign that says, 'Hey, look over here, I'm a murderer!'" AJ tilted his head to the side as he looked at her. "The best killers are also the best at disguising themselves as good people."

"I guess you're right about that. But I was right about Gill."

"I'm glad it worked out. Now about that dinner?"

"Soon, AJ." She smiled.

"Hm. Why does that sound like never?"

Blu leaned in close to him. For some ridiculous reason she couldn't resist. Her lips met his cheek in a soft lingering kiss. A sweet soft sigh emerged from between AJ's lips. "That's nice. But I still want dinner."

"Soon." Blu laughed as she chased the kids up the walkway to the parking lot.

They drove a few minutes down the road to a bakery. Blu parked and paraded the kids straight to the bathrooms to wash up before they had their treats. While she and Marley waited for Joey to emerge from the men's room, Blu surveyed the cupcake choices. The jingle of the bell over the door drew her attention. She turned to see Harry walking through the door.

"Harry." She smiled. "I guess you were right. You did see me again."

"Great timing. Any chance I can buy the cupcakes?" He waved to Joey as he stepped out of the restroom to join them.

"Sure." Blu nodded.

CHAPTER 27

As they ordered their cupcakes Blu studied Harry with increased interest. She still found it quite interesting that he'd been the one to take all the pictures of the ice cream shops.

"You'll be happy to know that they released Gill today."

"What?" Harry looked up at her sharply. "According to whom?"

"Oh. Well, the police chief told me. I'm going to see him in the morning. I know he's been thinking about selling the shop. I bet he would be very touched by the photographs you took, and the memory you shared with me."

"I bet." Harry smiled at the clerk and paid for the cupcakes. "Maybe I could go with you?"

"That's a wonderful idea." They sat together at a small table. "Do you think you could talk to him about maybe not selling the shop?"

"I could. If you want me to."

"Why is it so important what I want?" Blu asked.

"Why was it so important to you that Gill got out of jail?" Harry asked.

"Excuse me?"

"You were so certain. What about him made you so certain that he didn't deserve to be behind bars?"

"I guess because I feel that it's not his character to do something like that and definitely not to his wife."

"What do you know about his character?"

Blu frowned. "Did I say something to upset you?"

"No, I'm sorry. I have a bit of a mind for mystery. Sometimes I ask too many questions."

"Finish your cupcakes, kids."

Joey and Marley polished off their last few bites.

"I appreciate you spending some time with me, Blu. Here's my number. Please call me in the morning. I'd love to meet the man face-to-face."

"I'll call." Blu smiled at him.

That night when Blu tucked the kids into bed, she noticed that she was still waiting to feel calm. Everything in her mind told her that the crime was solved—that the right person was behind bars and everything would be fine. But something still left her feeling uneasy. As she fell asleep that night, her thoughts fixated on the small details of the crime. Although she couldn't place what it was, something didn't fit.

She woke the next morning to her cell phone ringing. "Hello?"

"Hey, it's Maddie. Sorry it's so early. I just wanted to see if you heard about Erica being arrested."

"Yes, I did. I was there. I'm sorry. I meant to call you about it."

"That's okay. It's been crazy. I'm just glad the police got the right person."

"I'm going to visit Gill this morning. Would you want to come along?"

"Sure."

"Oh, I have a friend that wants to join us too. The photographer—the one that took all the pictures of the ice cream shops."

"I still think that's a strange coincidence."

"Or maybe it's fate." Blu sat up in bed. "Either way, I hope that his pictures will sway Gill into keeping the shop open."

"Me too. I'm dying for some ice cream." Maddie gasped. "Oops—I'm sorry, that didn't come out the way I meant it."

"It's okay. Do you want to meet me at Gill's?"

"Sure, I can do that."

"I'll text you the address. I'm going to pick Harry up first."

"Sounds good."

Blu was relieved that she didn't have to rush into the kitchen. Rachel liked to make breakfast for the kids and watch cartoons with them on Saturday mornings. Blu usually had until about two to herself.

As she slipped out the side door to avoid a conversation, she nearly tripped over Joey's sneakers. That was when it struck her. The shoes. Why would Erica wear Gill's shoes? Was it just to frame the man? It seemed like an odd thing for the woman to choose to use to frame him.

It remained in her mind as she called Harry. He picked up on the first ring.

"Hi, Harry. I'm going over to Gill's. I wasn't sure if you had a car here, so I can pick you up if you'd like."

"Sure. I'm at Beachside Rooms. Do you know where it is?"

Blu's eyes widened. "Yes, I know exactly where it is."

"Great, see you in a few minutes."

Blu sat behind the wheel for a moment before she started the engine.

As she drove to Beachside Rooms she wondered if it could really be a coincidence that Harry and Erica were staying at the same place. Maybe the boarding house was running a special?

Harry waited for her outside. When she pulled up he opened the passenger side door.

"Good morning, Blu."

"Good morning."

He settled into the seat and looked over at her. "I brought my portfolio to show him."

"Great."

Blu drove toward Gill's house. When they arrived she

saw that Maddie's car was already there.

"Are we meeting someone else?" Harry frowned.

"Just my friend. She helped me prove Gill's innocence."

"Oh." He nodded. "Then she should be here too."

"Morning, Blu." Maddie gave her a quick hug, then the three of them walked up to the door.

"Mr. Peddle, are you in there?" Blu knocked on the door.

"Maybe we should go." Maddie frowned. "He hasn't opened the door for anyone. He didn't even come to the memorial wall."

"Mr. Peddle, please. It's me, Blu. I just want to talk to you. I have someone here who would like to meet you. I'm only here to help."

Harry nodded at her. "He'll open it. Just be patient."

Blu sighed. She hoped that Harry was right. So far his instincts had been pretty good.

A few minutes later the door to the small shop swung open. Mr. Peddle looked quite frail standing in the doorway.

"What is it? There's nothing that can be done for me."

"Mr. Peddle, I thought maybe if you could help me to understand a few things, we might be able to prove who really did this to your wife."

"What does it matter? It won't bring her back." He sighed so heavily that his entire body shook. "I'm alone now."

"It will keep you out of jail, Mr. Peddle."

He nodded his head and opened the door. "You can come in."

CHAPTER 28

Mr. Peddle turned and walked into the shop. Once the three filed in, he locked the door behind them. "Blu, I appreciate all that you're doing, but really it doesn't matter—whether I'm in prison or locked away in this empty shop. My life is over. Without Martha, I have nothing."

"That's not true. You have your shop and this community—and your reputation."

Gill hung his head. "No. Just go. I don't want anything to do with this anymore."

"But we figured out who killed Martha. Don't you want to know?"

Gill looked up at her words. He looked at each person who stood before him.

Harry reached up and adjusted his cap.

"Who was it?"

"A woman—Erica Grimes. She is the mother of one of your relatives that also owns an ice cream shop—Jarod Peddle."

"Jarod's mother?" Gill shook his head slowly. "No. That's not possible. She's a good woman. Why would she come after Martha? We made sure that she was taken care of, we made sure."

Blu's eyes widened. "I thought you said you didn't know Jarod?"

"Oh no, this is all wrong. You have to leave Erica out of this. She didn't know any better. She couldn't have killed Martha."

"But we have evidence that she was involved. She's been in town for the past few days. She was here when Martha was murdered. She must have been jealous of your love for Martha. She wanted you to be a father to Jarod." Blu tried to meet his eyes. "Did Martha know about him?"

"A father to Jarod? What are you talking about?" His eyes narrowed. "Are you accusing me of cheating on my wife, Blu? What a horrible thing to think!"

"I don't understand. If you didn't cheat on your wife, then why did you give him an ice cream shop? Why did you tell him that his father was dead?"

"His father is dead."

"No, he's not!" Harry whipped off his baseball cap and pulled out a gun.

Blu grabbed on to Maddie and pulled her away from the aim of the gun. "Stay back and stay calm," she whispered and held tightly to Maddie.

"Gill?" The anguish in the older man's voice was

audible, as was the shock.

Blu's mind raced. Gill and Martha had a son? Was that how all of the other Peddles were connected to him?

"That's what you always wanted, right? You never wanted me." Gill Junior glared at him. "I was nothing but a problem."

"Gill, that's not true. Your mother and I wanted you—every day of our lives we wanted you. We just didn't know how to help you. We wanted you to get the best help that you could."

"Don't lie to me!" The younger Gill waved the gun through the air. "I don't want to hear any more lies."

"Gill, please, this isn't right. These people did nothing to you. You have to let them go."

"No. I don't. They chose to come here—to your palace of lies—so they can stay. Do you know what it's been like for me? Living in hiding all this time?"

"If I'd known that you were alive I would have done anything to help you. Don't you know that none of this is your fault?"

Blu squeezed Maddie's hand and the two exchanged a quick look. They were in a tough situation with the front door locked and the back exit blocked by Gill Junior and the gun.

"Gill, your father didn't hurt your mother. No matter what you've heard." Blu tried to distract him from Gill Senior. "He's innocent."

"He's not innocent!" Gill roared. "He's not innocent

at all! He did this to me! All of this!"

"Gill. What did you do to your mother?" Gill Senior walked toward him. "What did you do to that sweet woman who did nothing but love you?"

"I didn't do anything that she didn't deserve. You both promised to be my family. You said that you'd take care of me, but you didn't!"

"Gill, we tried to get you help. You needed help. We tried counselors, therapies—even religion. You only seemed to become angrier—your mood swings more violent. Everywhere you went, you left a trail of hurt behind. You abandoned your children, children that didn't deserve that."

"Right. Not like me? So what if I didn't want to be a father?" He glared at Gill Senior. "I didn't have much of an example."

"Gill, I tried. Your mother tried too. But you were violent and we were afraid. We waited so long to have a child, maybe too long. If we had been younger—"

"No, you waited, and then you went to the baby store and you bought me. You didn't know that you couldn't return broken merchandise, did you?"

"It wasn't like that! You've got things all twisted up in your mind. You were six months old when we adopted you. We were so excited to finally have our son. We wanted you, Gill, we loved you. But we had a responsibility to make sure that you didn't hurt anyone. The doctors recommended inpatient therapy and we agreed to it—only to help you. When they told us that you'd died during your escape, your mother was heartbroken. So was I. You were our son. You are—" Mr. Peddle's voice cracked and he shook his head. "Oh, Gill, what have you done?"

Gill's hand trembled as he held the gun. "That wasn't it. You just didn't want me. You threw me away."

"No, son. It's your sickness telling you that. It's your sickness making you think that the people who loved you the most turned you away."

"You're wrong. You were supposed to pay too. That's why I came back here. The plan was for you to be blamed for her death. Then this one started nosing around." He jerked the gun toward Blu.

CHAPTER 29

Blu gasped and ducked away from the weapon.

"If it wasn't for her everything would have happened the way it was supposed to, and you would know what it was like to be locked away. I don't know how you got out of it, but I'm not going to let you get away with it."

"He didn't." Blu pulled away from Maddie. Maddie clung to her hand but Blu shook it free. "When Martha was found, he didn't try to get out of it. Your father confessed. I didn't understand it at the time, but now I do." Blu looked from the older man to the younger man. "You knew it was him, didn't you, Gill? You were trying to protect him, weren't you?"

"I didn't know how it was possible, but Martha told me that Jarod's mother came to her—that she knew that Gill Junior was still alive. She thought we knew too, and that we had lied to protect him. But we didn't know—not until then. When Martha died, I knew it had to be Gill. He tried it once before when he was a teenager. That was when we knew we had to act. He grew up knowing his mother was allergic to blueberries, but he put them in a smoothie and tried to get her to drink it. Why, Gill? Why her?" He met his son's eyes. "She was the best of all three of us."

"I don't know. I don't know!" Gill shook his head. "I don't know why I do the things I do."

"It's okay, Gill." The older man reached out to his son. "It's okay. It's not your fault. You didn't know. But now you do. Now you know that you're holding these innocent women hostage. It's time to let them go. All of this needs to end."

Gill Junior stared at his father. For just a moment Blu thought that he would surrender the gun. Instead, he raised it. He pointed it right at his father.

"No, don't!" Blu lunged toward him. She heard Maddie cry out in warning. Then Gill was on the ground before Blu had a chance to collide with him.

AJ had him pinned to the floor.

Blu moved fast and grabbed the gun from Gill's hand before he could use it.

"Stay down, Gill, stay down." Mr. Peddle crouched down beside his son.

Several police officers crammed their way into the ice cream shop. Blu stepped back as she watched Gill take his son's hand to offer him comfort. She was stunned that the man would be so gentle with the one who had taken Martha from him.

Maddie wrapped an arm around Blu and pulled her close. "Are you okay?"

"Yes. I am. I am now." Blu hugged her back.

AJ walked over to the two of them as Gill was led away by the officers.

His father followed after them.

"Blu, Maddie, are you hurt?" AJ looked between the two.

"I'm okay." Maddie nodded.

"We both are, thanks to you. How did you get in?"

"My uncle gave me a key. He wanted me to keep an eye on the ice cream shop during the investigation. When I saw what was happening through the window I came in as quietly as I could—just in time to see you about to tackle a man with a gun." He raised an eyebrow at Blu. "I'm pretty sure you intended to handle that yourself."

"I'm glad she didn't have to." Maddie sighed and rested her head on Blu's shoulder. "She might be a great nanny and a talented investigator, but you should have seen her in karate class."

"Oh?" AJ smiled. "I'd love to hear about that some time."

"I had coordination issues." Blu winced as she looked at Maddie. "Are you going to tell all my secrets?"

"Only the funny ones." Maddie grinned.

Blu sighed and then winked at Maddie. "I guess it's a small price to pay for our friendship."

"I'd love to hear everything." AJ grinned. "How about over dinner?" He met Blu's eyes.

"Soon, AJ. Soon."

"I'm going to hold you to that."

As AJ walked away Maddie elbowed Blu in the side. "What are you doing? He just saved your life. Have dinner with the man, for crying out loud."

"Summer doesn't last forever, Maddie."

"Maybe not, Blu, but one amazing summer can give you memories to enjoy for the rest of your life."

Blu thought about the scrapbooks sitting on the shelf in her room. Maybe Maddie was right. Maybe the memories were worth it.

When Blu reached her car she found Mr. Peddle waiting for her.

"Blu, thank you."

"I'm sorry, Gill. I don't understand what happened."

"Martha and I tried to have a child, but it never happened for us. We gave up on the idea. But then an opportunity came up to adopt a baby boy. We jumped at it. We loved Gill—I still do love him. But he had some problems, problems that weren't his fault. We tried to get him the best help we could. Then one day he threatened Martha. I couldn't tolerate that, so I sent him to a relative—then another relative and another. He tore through their lives like a tornado, leaving disaster everywhere he went. We just didn't have any luck."

"The horseshoe?"

"Yes it became a symbol for me. It was my way of showing Gill that I was never going to give up hope. I used the profits from this shop to open others for the people he hurt. I thought it was some small way to repay them. I made sure each one had a horseshoe. I wanted Gill to know that I was thinking of him, that he mattered to me."

Blu placed her hand on Mr. Peddle's arm as he continued.

"He hurt Erica the most. She thought she was in love. He got her pregnant and left her high and dry. Not long after that, we managed to get him committed for the third time in his life. He escaped one day and we were told he was swept away to his death. I guess Erica found out he was still alive, because he tried to buy the shop we gave to her son. She thought we knew all along. It took Martha some time to convince her that we didn't." Gill wiped at his eyes. "We really loved him. Martha would have done anything for him."

"I know you did, Gill," said Blu.

"The only comfort I take in all of this is that Martha passed away thinking that she had reunited with him. I'm sure she never knew he put the blueberry sauce in her ice cream." He shook his head. "Blu, children are beautiful. I love having my shop, I love seeing all the children come and go, but some are broken in ways that can't be fixed. Gill was one of those children. Yet, somehow I didn't love him any less."

"He was lucky to have you. I'm sorry that this happened to you. Is that why you confessed?"

"I knew it had to be Gill when I found out how she

died. I figured I only have a little time left, and this was one last way I could help my son, but now I know better. He would have continued to hurt people." He sighed. "I just don't know what to do."

"May I make a suggestion?" Blu met his eyes.

"What is it?" He looked back at her.

"Keep your shop open. Be a little bit of light in every child's life. Be the good memory that sticks with them forever. You do so much just by doing that."

"Maybe I will, Blu." He nodded. "Maybe I will."

"I don't know if ever told you this, but I visited your shop once when I was a kid—with my whole family. It has been a beautiful memory for me my entire life—all because of you."

"Thanks. I appreciate that. I think I'll spend some time at the memorial wall tonight."

"I'll join you, if that's okay."

"That would be wonderful." He smiled.

Blu thought for just a second that she could see a spark of hope in his eyes.

CHAPTER 30

That night when Blu arrived at the Beach Bum to spend some time at the memorial wall, she was astounded by the large number of photographs that were displayed. Her eyes brimmed with tears the moment she saw Gill, who stood in front of all of them.

She walked up beside him. "Isn't it amazing?"

"Yes. Yes it is." He nodded. "I've been looking at all of the pictures. The funny thing is, you'd think with all the faces and all the time that's passed, I wouldn't remember any of them. But I do. I can even remember what most ordered. These were my happy memories too—our happy memories." He smiled at the picture of Martha at the top of the wall. "She was the kindest woman in the world. Gill could not have had a better mother."

Blu wrapped her arm around his shoulders. "You are an amazing man."

"I hope that I can be without her. You should look at the pictures. There's one that's rather familiar to me—a double chocolate peanut butter swirl with sprinkles on top."

Blu raised an eyebrow. "That sounds delicious."

"I thought you might think so. Take a look."

As he walked away, Blu scanned the photographs. She wasn't sure exactly what she was looking for, but she was intrigued. There were pictures of families, single people, sports teams, and even a group of service dogs who were treated to special ice cream for dogs. Blu thought each picture was lovely, but nothing stood out to her as familiar.

Then she saw it, nestled in the middle of all of the other photographs. It was a picture of her as a child. Her eyes widened at the sight. She had a dab of ice cream on her nose. All at once she remembered the exact order she'd given to Mr. Peddle that day—a double chocolate peanut butter swirl with sprinkles on top. She shook her head and laughed.

"Whose picture could this be?" She reached for it to see if there was anything written on the back.

"Don't touch the photographs, Blu." AJ leaned against the table behind her, with a big grin on his face. "Look with your eyes, not with your hands."

Blu shot a look over her shoulder at him. "I was just curious about who this photograph might belong to."

"Why?" AJ looked into her eyes.

Blu returned his gaze. "Do you know who put this picture on the wall?"

He folded his arms across his chest. "Maybe."

"AJ."

"Blu." He grinned.

"Stop teasing me. I want to know."

"Why?"

"AJ!"

"Okay, okay. It's my picture. I put it on the wall."

"What?" Blu stared at him. "How is that possible?"

"Uh, I took a picture. When I was a kid the local newspaper had this contest one summer—to take as many summer photographs as we could. I saw this girl—she was seriously chowing down on her ice cream cone. She had it all over her face. I thought it couldn't get more summer than that, so I took her picture. I don't know, it sounds weird now, but at the time I thought she was probably the most beautiful thing about that summer."

Blu raised an eyebrow. "Are you toying with me, AJ?"

"Huh?" He rubbed the back of his neck. "What's wrong? It's just an old picture."

"Are you telling me that you have no idea who the girl is in that picture?"

"Should I?" He shrugged. "I never saw her again after that summer. I spent the whole time trying to get her attention, but she never gave me a second glance."

Blu's heart raced. She looked back at the picture. Was that why AJ was so familiar to her? Could she have remembered him from all those years before?

"Are you okay? You look a little pale."

"AJ, that's me." Blu's lips quirked upward into a smile. "You took a picture of me."

AJ laughed and shook his head. "That's not possible."

"I wouldn't think so either, but it is me. I'm that young girl in the picture."

"If you say it's you, I believe you. In fact, I'm not sure why I didn't see it for myself." AJ's grin grew wider.

"See what?"

"You're still the most beautiful thing about summer."

ALL TITLES BY MACI GRANT

http://Amazon.com/author/macigrant
*Check the author page for current list of titles

Summer in Diamond Bay